'Who was at the door just now?'

It seemed the summons had not been necessary. Lillian was standing on the main staircase. She looked as beautiful as he remembered—and as enigmatic. Gerry felt the same tightening in his throat that had come upon him the day they'd met. This time he fought against it. While it might be fashionable to moon over another man's wife, it did not do to be so affected by one's own.

He straightened to parade-perfect attention, then grinned up at her.

'No one in particular. Merely your husband, madam.'

Her head snapped up to see him. Her face shuttled through half a dozen expressions, trying to settle on one that could both express her emotions and welcome him properly. He was pretty sure that none of what he saw resembled gratitude or joy. But before any of it could truly register her knees began to fold under her.

Author Note

When working on this book I spent a lot of time researching the popular pastimes of a gentleman's house party. I am not much of a card player myself. Actually, I'm not much of a pool player either. But I found the changes in the game of billiards to be really interesting.

First, we are talking proper British billiards—with red and white balls as opposed to the multi-coloured rack that we Americans use. These balls began as wood, which would have been uneven and hard to use. If Gerry Wiscombe learned to play with those, they were household antiques. By the Regency everyone was using ivory.

The table he played on would have been made of wood, not slate. To minimise warping, the surface under the felt was made with strips of wood, with the grains going in different directions. This was covered by baize, which needed to be ironed before each game to remove the wrinkles. There would have been a special iron in the room for this, which our cheating Ronald in this story has not used.

And although by the Regency almost everyone had switched to using a cue, the original stick had a clubbed end and was called a mace. It was difficult to use for some shots, and serious players would turn it around and use the pointed end. Eventually everyone decided that the handle was better than the clubbed head, and that's how we got cues.

Thanks for reading!

THE SECRETS OF WISCOMBE CHASE

Christine Merrill

MILLS & BOON®

First published in Great Britain 2016
By Mills & Boon, an imprint of HarperCollins*Publishers*
1 London Bridge Street, London, SE1 9GF

Large Print edition 2016

ISBN: 978-0-263-26302-2

Our policy is to use papers that are natural, renewable and recyclable products and made from wood grown in sustainable forests. The logging and manufacturing processes conform to the legal environmental regulations of the country of origin.

Printed and bound in Great Britain
by CPI Antony Rowe, Chippenham, Wiltshire

Christine Merrill lives on a farm in Wisconsin, USA, with her husband, two sons, and too many pets—all of whom would like her to get off of the computer so they can check their e-mail. She has worked by turns in theatre costuming and as a librarian. Writing historical romance combines her love of good stories and fancy dress with her ability to stare out of the window and make stuff up.

To Kevin McElroy and Wayne White.
Congratulations from someone
who knew you when…

'Love is something eternal.
The aspect may change, but not the essence.'
—Vincent van Gogh

Chapter One

'Miss North, would you do me the honour of accepting my hand in holy matrimony?'

Lillian North did her best to smile at the unfortunate boy kneeling before her on the parlour rug and readied herself for the only answer she would be permitted to give.

Once, she had harboured illusions about love and romance. Most young girls did. But they had been left in the nursery, along with the other spectacular fictions about fairy princesses and brave knights riding to their rescue. When she'd made her come-out, Father and Ronald had explained the way the world truly worked.

It was her job to be pretty, pleasant and biddable, and attract what offers she could from gentlemen of the *ton*. In the end, she would marry and marry well. But it would be to a man of Father's choosing and she was not to question the choice.

She had been in London for months, both this year and last. She had danced at Almack's until her slippers were near to worn through. She had smiled until her cheeks ached with it and been so agreeable that people must think her simple in the head. It felt as if she had been introduced to every eligible man in Britain. While she'd her favourites, she had not allowed herself to form an attachment to any of them. She must never forget that the final choice would not be hers.

She had done as she was told and cast the properly baited net as wide as possible. When the time was right, her father and brother would draw it in to evaluate the catch. They would throw back the unworthy and keep no more than two or three of the very best. Then, the serious negotiating would begin. In the end, she would be decked in flowers and sent up the aisle of St George's to stand at the side of a scion of the nobility. Father had assured her that he would settle for nothing less than a London cathedral and a groom that would leave other girls green at her success.

But now, all the plans and the manoeuvring of a season and a half were for naught. Without warning, she had been hauled out of town and informed that the choice had been made. She was to marry Gerald Wiscombe.

And who was he? It was as if she had cast her net and brought in a dark horse. Her metaphors were as muddled as her thoughts, but she could hardly be blamed for confusion. Mr Wiscombe was a total stranger to her. Although he was not a particularly memorable fellow, she was sure she'd have recalled meeting him, if only because he was unlike any of the men who'd courted her in London.

Lily had prayed each night that her future husband would have admirable qualities beyond wealth and station. Perhaps a love match was unrealistic. But, her future would be happier if it was, at least, founded on mutual respect. When she had taken the time to search for them, she had found good qualities in each of the men who had escorted her. Why, then, could she find nothing to recommend her father's final choice?

To begin with, Mr Wiscombe was too young to be taken seriously. He was barely into his majority, only a year or so older than her. He was not even out of university and more interested in his impending Tripos in Mathematics than wedding her. In fact, he'd refused to come to London and court her. She had been expected to go to Cambridge to see him, so that the burden of this proposal would not interrupt his studies.

It did Mr Wiscombe no credit that he augmented his youth and uninterest with a lack of fashion and an awkwardness of address. Where was the evidence of his precious education? There was no sign on his soft, round face that he was destined to be a wit or a wag. When he smiled, the gap in his front teeth made him look as simple as she felt.

Looks were not important, she reminded herself. After dancing with men old enough to sire her, she had steeled herself to ignore appearances. Brains were not necessary if one had rank or money.

But that still did not explain Gerald Wiscombe. A few short weeks ago, Father had turned up his nose at an interested baronet as being too low-born to qualify as son-in-law. But now, there was nothing more than a 'mister' rocking uneasily on his knees in the parlour of a roadside inn, awaiting the answer.

He must be quite wealthy to make up for the lack of a title. But Mr Wiscombe had not bought so much as a bottle of wine to celebrate this day, nor had he visited a tailor to impress her. The cuffs of his coat were worn and one of the unpolished buttons clung to the garment by its last thread.

'I do not have much,' he said, affirming her worst fears. 'I have no family to speak of. None at all, actually. I am the last of the Wiscombes. And the family fortune was gone a generation ago.'

'I am sorry to hear it,' she said, not so much sorry as totally perplexed.

'Of course, Wiscombe Chase is lovely.'

A country manor? She smiled encouragingly.

'Was lovely,' he corrected with a shrug and a frown, as though he'd meant to lie and could not quite get it to stick. 'It needs much work and the loving hand of a woman.'

Which probably meant it was a mouldering

ruin and he was seeking a rich wife to repair it for him. This man was the polar opposite of the one she had been sent out to catch.

At some point, Father's agenda had changed and she had not been informed. But when was Father not hatching a plan of some kind? His schemes invariably left him better off than he had been, while those who had dealings with him always seemed surprised to be poorer and less successful. Even so, few of them would have called him swindler. Those who lost to him preferred to think of him as that dashed, lucky Mr North.

She had always been inside the invisible boundary that separated her family from the rest of the world. No matter how precarious things might seem, everything would go well for her in the end. Because she was a North.

Until today, at least.

Did her father not understand that a young lady's reputation was a fragile thing? Marriage was a permanent and nigh unbreakable contract. He could not barter her out of the family only to pull her back on some tenuous legal string, like the Bolivian emerald mine she'd seen him sell at a profit some three times already.

Worse yet, she was alone in her ignorance. Her brother, Ronald, had baulked when forced to escort her about London on the hunt for a suitable match. But he had been the one to introduce Mr Wiscombe and seemed as eager to see her married as Father did.

'Miss North?' Mr Wiscombe prompted, noticing the long and doubtful silence that had followed his offer.

She looked down at what was likely to be her future husband. He was staring up at her, mouth gaping slightly. He reminded her of a barely formed chick, unfledged, inexperienced and waiting to be fed. She feared the young *avis Wiscombe* was about to be pushed early from the nest and gobbled by waiting predators, *genus North.*

It made his next statement all the more worrying.

'I wouldn't bother you, if that's what you are afraid of.' Now he was blushing. 'We need time to get to know each other, before that. Your father has promised to buy me a commission so I might make my fortune. I will be gone for some years. When I am returned there will be enough money for the two of us to live quite well. And then...'

The mystery deepened. First off, he'd said the word *bother* with such significance that she assumed he meant something. And he assumed she understood. She supposed she did, after a fashion. He must be talking about what occurred between a husband and wife. She had no mother to explain details to her and was far too afraid and embarrassed to ask Father. If it was bothersome, she was not sure she wished to know the specifics.

But if he meant to join the army at her father's bequest and be gone for several years? That was simply laughable. She doubted Gerald Wiscombe would last several minutes before the French, much less several years. Did her father mean to send this poor boy to his doom?

She did not want to believe it. While her father was somewhat less than honest, she had never known him to be brutal. But the harder she tried to reject it the more her mind filled with the icy certainty that this was precisely what Phineas

North intended. If he was willing to sacrifice his own daughter like a chess piece, what hope did this poor young man have to survive until checkmate?

If that was the game, then she refused to play her part in it. It would be a lie to say that she felt affection for the man in front of her. But neither did she wish him ill. Even if she felt nothing at all, how could she live with herself if the marriage was little more than a death sentence for her husband? She would not be permitted to refuse. But perhaps if she could get Mr Wiscombe to withdraw the offer, the matter would settle itself.

Lily wet her lips. 'Are you sure that is wise?'

He was blinking at her as if he had no idea what she meant. Perhaps he was not quite right in the head.

'The army will be very dangerous.' She spoke slowly, so he could understand. When this did not seem to make an impression, she added, with additional emphasis, 'There is no guarantee that you will return in a few years with a fortune. In fact, there is no guarantee that you will return at all.'

In response, he blinked the watery grey eyes in his round face and gave her another foolish grin.

'You might be killed,' she said. Now her voice sounded testy. She did not wish to be cross with him, but he needn't be so stupid, either. She shouldn't have to spell out the trap he was walking into.

Finally, one doughy hand reached out to cover hers. 'You need not worry about that. It is a possibility, of course. But there are many others equally grim. I might fall off my horse and break my neck before we can even say the vows. Or get struck by lightning while picking flowers in the garden. Or I might survive the battle and live to a ripe old age.' He blinked again. 'You are not afraid of that, are you?'

Afraid? Why should she be afraid of such an unlikely possibility?

Now he was looking at her as though she were the one who did not understand the gravity of the situation. Suddenly, she was sure that, all this time, he had been measuring her just as she had measured him. 'You do understand, if you are to marry me, it will be till death us do part,' he said and paused to let the words sink in. 'Although you obviously assume otherwise, my death may be a long time in coming.'

Did he think her so stupid that she did not understand the basic vows she would be taking? Or had he just insulted her, hinting that she was marrying him in the hopes that he would die? It would be too horrible, if there weren't some truth to it.

He was still blinking at her with those innocent, wet eyes. There was something hiding deep within them and it was not the eagerness of a bridegroom. The light shining there was like the sun reflected off cold iron. What he felt when he looked at her was not passion, or even affection. It was grim resolve.

His words had been a last attempt to make her prove her worth and admit that she had no desire to marry him. If she said yes to his proposal, he would assume she was as grasping and sly as the rest of her family, and meant to lure him into a marriage with the hope of imminent widowhood.

She stiffened. Any other girl would have withdrawn her hand and rejected his suit without another thought. She'd have cut him dead, had there been any chance that they would ever meet again, which they would not. If he liked his mathematics books so well, he could marry them. She would go back to the handsome, titled men of Almack's and forget him utterly. He could return to his ruin of a house. Once there, he could lick his wounds and brood upon this day with the embarrassment it deserved.

But she was not any other girl. She was the daughter of Phineas North. If she left the room after refusing Mr Wiscombe, Father would turn her back at the doorstep to hear him again. Should she manage to escape to her room, she would be locked there until she came to her senses and did as she was told. If the current plan fell through and she was able to divest herself of Gerald Wiscombe, there was no guarantee that the next choice she was offered would be any better. In fact, it could be much, much worse.

She was as trapped and doomed as the boy on his knees before her. So she looked down at him with what she hoped was an aloof, but ultimately benevolent stare. 'I am well aware of the words of the marriage ceremony, Mr Wiscombe, and have enough wit to understand their meaning. If we marry, it is for life. However long—' she gave him another probing, significant look '—or short that might be. I am also aware that it gives you the right to, as you put it earlier, bother me whenever you so choose to do so. But if you do not have the sense to be afraid of Napoleon, than why should I be afraid of marrying you?'

For a moment, everything changed and not for the better. He favoured her with the gap-toothed grin of an idiot. Then he rose to his feet. Rather than attempting to kiss her, he clasped her hand in a firm, manly shake. 'Very well. It is a bargain, then. We will be married as soon as your father can arrange for the licence. When I return from the Peninsula, we will begin our future together.'

The poor fool. What else could she do but nod in agreement? Once he was gone, perhaps she could persuade Ronald to tell her what was really going on. But there was one thing that she already knew. If Gerald Wiscombe had chosen to make a bargain with her father, his future and fortune were decided and fate was laughing in his face.

Chapter Two

'If you are intent on selling your commission, Wiscombe, we shall be sad to see you go. It was a fortuitous day for the British army when you first decided to take up the sword.'

'Thank you, Colonel Kincaid.' Gerry dipped his head in modest acknowledgement to the man seated at the desk. Whenever he received such compliments, he was always faintly relieved that his commanding officers had not been present on the day, seven years ago, that he'd made that decision. It had been an act of desperation, pure and simple. There had been nothing the least bit heroic about it.

'It is a shame you do not wish to continue in the service. Surely we could find a place for an officer with such a past as yours.'

The thought had crossed his mind. Even as he passed through the arched gate of the Horse Guards, he had considered asking for another posting. A few years in India would not go amiss. But after so much time away, avoiding his home felt more like cowardice than bravery.

Gerry looked Kincaid square in the eye to show that he would not be moved. 'It would be an honour to continue in service to the crown. But after seven years, it is time to trade one war for another.'

The colonel gave him the same mildly confused look that others had given him when he had phrased it so. It did not matter. Understanding was not necessary. He smiled back at the man to show that it was all in jest. 'It is a long time to be away from home. When I left, I was but newly married.' He opened the locket he carried that contained the miniature of Lillian.

The colonel smiled back and gave him a knowing wink. 'I see. There is little the army can offer that can compete with the open arms of a beautiful woman waiting eagerly for your return.'

Gerry nodded again. She had been beautiful. Likely, she still was. The position of her arms and her degree of eagerness were yet to be de-termined. His smile remained unwavering, as the papers were signed that severed him from the military.

From Whitehall, he went to Bond Street to find a tailor. He shuddered to think what cloth-ing was still in the cupboards of his old room. He'd been a half-formed boy when he'd left the place to go to Portugal. Even if the coats still fit, they would be even more threadbare and out of fashion than they had been when he'd left. After Father had died, he'd had not a penny to spare on his appearance. But there was no need to spend the rest of his life in uniform, now that he had earned enough to pay for proper clothing.

His dragoon's regimentals were more than impressive enough to turn heads as he walked down the street. He heard the whispers that fol-lowed him as he passed the shops.

'Is that Wiscombe?'

'There he is.'

'Captain Wiscombe. Hero of Salamanca. Hero of Waterloo.'

Had the word of his return reached Wiscombe Chase? It must have, if strangers could recognise him on the street. What would North's reaction be when Gerry turned up to reclaim his home, after all this time?

And what would *she* think of it?

He turned his mind away from that question and ordered the new clothes sent on ahead of him. Then he turned his horse to the north and began the ride home.

Once he was clear of the city, he gave Satan his head and let the miles pass uncounted. This was how it should be, man and steed travelling light. When the beast tired, they stopped and slept rough, not bothering with an inn. When it rained, Gerry threw an oilcloth over his coat and let the water run off him in sheets. Later, the sun returned and dried them, filling his nostrils with the smell of steaming wool and horse.

Kincaid had been right. He would miss this. But the whole point in buying a commission had been to gain the money to save the house and secure his future. He'd succeeded in that some years past. After Vitoria, there had been more than enough money to clear his debts, fix the roof and have a tidy sum left to invest.

He could have gone home then. But he had not. Even after Boney was sent to Elba, he had dawdled. The little Frenchman's escape had come as a relief, for it meant a few more months during which he could delay the inevitable.

Now that the last shot had been fired and Napoleon was off to St Helena, he was out of excuses. It was time to return to his first responsibility.

And there, on the horizon, was the stone marker that indicated the beginning of the Wiscombe family land. His land, he amended. There had been no family living when he had taken up the sword. If there had been anyone left, the cowardly boy he had been would have appealed to them for help and avoided the next seven years of his own life.

Gerry shrugged at the thought and the horse under him sensed his unease and gave a faint shift of his own.

He stroked the great black neck and they continued on the road that wound through the dense wood surrounding the house. The wild, untamed nature of the property was more beautiful than any formal garden. Beautiful, but useless. Dense woodland was bordered on one side by rills and streams too small to navigate by boat and on the other by granite tors and bogs that made coach travel impossible.

His life might have been easier had his ancestors settled in a place capable of sustaining crops, cattle or industry. The land around Wiscombe Chase was fit for nothing but hunting. Since he did not intend to ever take another life, animal or human, it might be better to sell the lot to a sportsman who could appreciate it.

But after all the blood he had shed to keep it, he could not bring himself to entertain the idea. Some men at his side had fought for king and country. Others hated the French tyrant more than they loved their own cause. Still others wanted money or glory.

He had fought for his birthright. This ten square miles of wood and moor was his own country to defend and rule. It generated not a penny of income. If he was honest, he did not even like the draughty and impractical manor that had drained away the Wiscombe fortune. But, by God, it was his, to the last rock.

As if to confirm the wisdom of his decision,

he saw a shift in the leaves on the left side of the road. He reined in and warned Satan to be still. A twig cracked and he held his breath, waiting. The stag stepped into the road, watching him as intently as he watched it. The spread of the antlers was broader than he remembered and the muzzle had more grey in it. But the left shoulder had the same scrape from his father's bullet, so very long ago.

'Hello, old friend,' he whispered.

The deer gave a single snort, then tossed his head and disappeared into the trees.

In response, Gerry's heart leapt with joy at the rightness of being home. Though he'd fought against it since the day he'd left, he belonged here. He spurred the horse to clear the last stand of trees and the house came into sight.

It had been near to ruin when he'd left. But now the heavy brown stone was clean and the roof sported new grey slate. The windows sparkled bright in the growing dusk. And every last one of them was lit.

Perhaps they had filled the house to the rafters with friends to welcome him home. He could not help the ironic smile this idea brought. He'd had no friends at all when he'd left England. To the best of his knowledge, that had not changed in his absence.

It likely meant that he was interrupting someone else's party. He felt the same unholy glee that sometimes took him when charging on to the battlefield. It had never been the carnage that attracted him. It was the clarity that came when one knew life might end at any moment. Other fears paled in comparison, especially the fear of one's own mistakes. He had learned to act before he was acted upon. After years of being life's pawn, he had become the force of chaos that acted upon others.

He smiled. If ever there was an opposing army deserving of chaotic upset, it was the North family.

He cantered the last half mile, coming to an easy stop at the front door. The footman who came forward to take the horse did not know him. But then, in '08, he had not been able to afford a servant at the door, much less the livery that this boy wore.

His butler had no such problems with recognition. The door opened and the expression on the man's normally impassive face changed to surprise. 'Master Gerald?' Those words were smothered with a quick clearing of the throat and 'Begging your pardon, Captain Wiscombe.' But underneath the reserve, he was near to grinning, and so proud of his master that he looked ready to pop his waistcoat buttons.

Gerry had no reason for reserve with the man who had comforted him on the night his father had died. 'Aston.' He reached forward and offered a brief, manly embrace, clasping the fellow's shoulder and patting him once on the back. 'It is good to be home.'

'And to have you home as well, sir. We have followed your exploits in the newspapers. It was very exciting.'

So they had heard of him here. Of course they had. Who had not? All the same, he was glad to have worn his uniform so that he might reinforce the image of returned war hero. Even after days in the saddle, the short jacket and shiny boots were more than a little impressive. And the sword at his side was proof that he was no idle fop in feathers and braid.

Aston looked past him. 'Are you unaccompanied? Where is the luggage?'

'Arriving later. I had it sent, direct from London.' He smiled at the old servant. 'I did not wish to wait for it.'

The man nodded back, taking his haste for a compliment. 'We are all glad that you did not.'

Was that true above stairs as well as below? He sincerely doubted it. 'Where is she?' he said softly, looking past the butler. 'Not waiting at the door for my return, I see.'

'Come into the house, Captain.' The man was still grinning over the new rank. 'While you refresh yourself, I will find Mrs Wiscombe.'

'Aston? Who was at the door, just now?'

It seemed the summons was not necessary. Lillian was standing on the main staircase. She looked as beautiful as he remembered and as enigmatic. He felt the same tightening in his throat that had come upon him the day they'd met. This time, he fought against it. While it might be fashionable to moon over another man's wife, it did not do to be so affected by one's own.

He straightened to parade-perfect attention,

then looked up at her. 'No one in particular. Merely your husband, madam.'

Her head snapped up to see him. Her face shuttled through a half-dozen expressions, trying to settle on the one that could both express her emotions and welcome him properly. He was pretty sure that none of what he saw resembled gratitude or joy. But before any of it could truly register, she gave up and her eyes rolled back as her knees began to fold under her.

'Bugger.' He lunged forward, putting his battlefield reflexes to good use, and caught her before she could reach the ground. The woman in his arms was heavier than she'd appeared at the altar. Hardly a surprise. He had changed, as well. But she was not too heavy. Had he found her in Portugal, he'd have described her to his mates as a 'tidy armful'.

'The bench, Captain.' The butler gestured to a place beside the stairs.

'The sitting room,' Gerry corrected.

'I will send for madam's maid with the hartshorn.'

'Nonsense,' Gerry announced, carrying his wife through the open sitting-room doors to a divan by the fire. 'She just needs to get the blood back to her head.' He settled Lillian on the sofa and sat at the opposite end, taking her feet into his lap to elevate them.

The feel of her dainty slippers against his thighs did more to redirect his blood flow than hers. He snatched a pillow from behind him and slipped it beneath them to give her more height and him a chance to regain his sanity.

Her eyelids fluttered, the long lashes revealing flashes of eyes as soft and brown as a doe's. It must have been God's own joke to give such an innocent face to a woman like Lillian North.

He smiled to hide his thoughts. 'There. See? It is working already. Fetch her a ratafia, or some other restorative.' Damn it all, he could use a stiff brandy himself. But he needed a clear head if he was to stand against the Norths, so he asked for nothing.

His wife was fully awake now. When she realised her position, she hurriedly pulled up her feet and righted herself, swaying slightly on the cushion beside him as she tried to regain her poise.

'Easy,' he cautioned. 'Do not rush or you will become dizzy again.'

'You startled me,' she said, rubbing her temple as if her head ached. More likely, it was to shield her face so she did not have to look him in the eye.

So she was startled. How unfortunate. Even though she had not expected to see him again after their wedding breakfast, she must have heard of him in these past years. It had probably vexed her and her family to find him so stubbornly hard to kill.

The butler signalled the footman, who stepped forward with a glass. Gerry pressed it into her hand.

She drank deeply, as though desperate for anything that gave her an excuse not to talk.

'So it shocked you to unconsciousness to see me again,' he prompted, enjoying her discomfort.

'I was aware that you had returned to England. But if you had notified us of your impending arrival, the house might have been prepared for you.' She had the nerve to sound annoyed with him.

He smiled all the wider. 'In my time away, I've learned to value the element of surprise.'

'I must tell the servants to air out your room.' She set aside her glass and made to stand up.

'No need.' He grinned at her and took her hand, pulling her none too gently back to the seat next to him. 'They saw my arrival and are most likely doing so without your instruction. I am sure they would not expect you to leave my side so soon after our reunion. We have been apart for ages. We have much to discuss.'

She looked so miserable at the thought of their impending talk that he almost pitied her. Then he remembered that she had earned any misery a hundredfold for the way she had treated him.

Before they could begin, they were interrupted by voices in the hallway. A man and boy were coming towards the sitting room in animated conversation about the quality of the trout they had caught for tonight's dinner.

In truth, it was the younger one that did most of the talking. The man with him answered in annoyed monosyllables before shouting, 'Aston! What would it take for a man to get a drink before dinner? And what the devil is all the ruckus about? The rest of the party is not yet back from their hunt, but servants are running around as if the house is on fire.'

Lillian's eyes widened and she looked ready to call out a warning.

Gerry laid a hand on her arm to silence her. Then he spoke in a voice that carried easily to the hall. 'You have but to ask the lord of the manor, Ronald North. Or have you been playing that role yourself, in my absence?' He'd meant it to sound joking, but it came out as an accusation. Gerry softened the words with his most innocuous smile, as his wife's brother appeared suddenly in the doorway and braced a hand against the frame as if to steady himself.

'Wiscombe.' Though his voice had been clear and jovial a moment before, now Ronald seemed winded. He looked even more shocked than his sister had been.

Gerry took care to hide the malice he felt behind a wide-eyed, innocent look. 'What a surprise to come home and find you still in my house.'

'Surprise?' The man stammered over the word, still trying to decide what his reaction should be.

'Well, not really,' Gerry added, his grin broadening. 'Of course I expected to find you here. I gave you permission to live here in my absence. But there appears to be a house party in residence. Is it to honour my return? You must have heard of my homecoming and gathered my friends to welcome me.'

'Of course.' Ronald leapt for the lifeline he'd been offered, clinging to it for all he was worth. 'When we heard that you had survived Waterloo...' He gave a capacious wave of his hand to encompass the frenzied celebration that his success had caused. From one who had no right to set the comings and goings of the household it was more than a little presumptuous.

'It was a dashed piece of good luck that I am here at all,' Gerry answered him, with a pleased nod. 'I've been within ames ace of coming home in a box so many times over the years that I quite lost count.'

'How did you manage to survive?' By his tone, Ronald North was annoyed that he had done so.

Gerry shrugged. 'I suspect it was the prayers of my lovely wife that did it. There always seemed to be an angel who could grab me by the col-

lar and pull me back from the brink.' He gave
a deliberately expansive wave of his hand and
jostled the glass Lillian had been holding, sending a splash of her drink on to the rug.

'I suspect so.' Ronald was staring at him intently as if wondering whether he might still be
the lucky idiot they wanted him to be. Gerry
smiled back, doing his best to look harmless.
Let him think what he liked. Better yet, let him
think what Gerry meant him to.

'But Waterloo is several months passed,' Gerry
continued. 'Do not say you have been rejoicing
all this time without me. Judging by the red in
your nose, the cellar must be quite empty by
now.' The same years that had toughened Gerry
had softened his wife's brother. The chestnut
hair he shared with his sister had lost its lus-
tre. His waist had thickened and his face was
bloated from over-indulgence. In school, Ronald had been a handsome fellow with an easy
manner and enough blunt in his pocket to ensure
his popularity. But now it was hard to see his
brother-in-law as anything other than the disso-
lute wastrel he had been even then.

'You need not fear that the house is dry,' Ronald said, matching his tone to Gerald's. 'Your cellar is excellent, Wiscombe. I know, for I stocked it myself. And the guests that are here for your arrival?' He gave another flourish of his hand. 'The cream of London society, dear boy. The very pinnacle.'

'The pinnacle? Then they are likely strangers to me.' He'd been a young nobody when he'd left for Portugal, well beneath the notice of the *ton*. It had flattered him that Ronald North might think him a fit match for his beautiful sister. He had been a fool. He gave Ronald another empty-headed smile to prove nothing had changed. 'But I am sure we will get on well. The chaps in my regiment said as long as I was paying for the wine I was very good company.'

He felt his wife tense next to him as she recognised the sarcasm that her brother had missed. Even at their first meeting, she had been better at reading him than either of the other Norths. It was a shame that her character was not equal to her intelligence.

'You will meet the guests over dinner,' Ronald said, smiling back. Apparently, he was also oblivious to the fact that it was not his place to be issuing such assurances to the man who owned the house.

'I must change the seating at the table,' Lily added, trying to escape him again.

Gerry pulled her down again. 'Aston will have told the housekeeper by now. Mrs Fitz is quite capable of rearranging a few chairs.' He gave her a smile that would have terrified her, had she known him better.

Perhaps she did know him. He felt another tremor in the muslin-draped leg resting against his. He dropped a hand on to her twitching knee in an overly familiar gesture of comfort and she stilled. But it was not a sign of calm so much as the terrified immobility of a rabbit before a hawk.

For now, he ignored her and her brother as well, staring towards the hall. 'Never mind them. There is but one person here I truly wish to meet.' He raised his finger to point towards the shadow hovering in the doorway behind Ronald North. 'Come forth. Let me get a look at you.'

The boy stepped forward from around Ronald's legs and walked into the room. He looked at Gerry with none of the nervous suspicion of the two adults in the room. But what reason would he have to fear this stranger? Especially since he had been eavesdropping on the conversation and must be aware who he was about to meet.

Gerry saw the lightning-fast glance that passed between the siblings as the boy stepped forward and they sought the words to cover this situation in a single shared look.

Once again he had the element of surprise. He pressed his advantage and sprang the ambush before they could speak. 'As if I could not discover with my own eyes who this must be. Come forward, boy. Meet your father, returned from the wars.'

Chapter Three

Lily was going to faint again. She could see the black dots gathering before her eyes as Stewart stepped forward towards Captain Wiscombe's outstretched hand. Now, of all times, she must not lose her senses. The dizziness came from holding one's breath and denying oneself of air. It was a bad habit of hers and she must learn to break it if she did not want to appear frail and unworthy to her heroic spouse. She forced herself to take the breath that would clear her head. The resulting gasp was loud enough to be heard by the entire room.

Stewart started like a rabbit. But Captain Wiscombe ignored it, even though he must have felt the couch shake with her quaking knees.

She had nothing to fear in this meeting, or so

she'd been telling herself for most of the past seven years. Before he had left her, Mr Wiscombe had been kindness itself. He had been gentle with her, considerate of her feelings and almost as frightened of the idea of marriage to her as she'd been of his chances in the army. The Gerald Wiscombe she remembered had been more likely to be harmed than to cause harm to another. She would explain to Gerald what had happened. He would understand and arrange a quiet separation.

But it was foolish to think of the man beside her as the same person who had left. He had not just been transformed by experience. He had been transmuted into another being. There was nothing left of the pudgy, scholarly boy who had stammered out a proposal to her. The soft brown hair had burned blond in sunlight and wind had given it a casual wave. In contrast, the skin of his face had darkened and the features had sharpened to a hawk nose and cleft chin. The grey eyes set beneath his furrowed brow were bright and as hard as flint.

He was still wearing the dashing red coat of a dragoon, with gold at shoulder and sleeve.

And somewhere, there had to be a sword. By the resolute look on this man's face, it had seen good use. If he decided to punish those who had wronged him...

'Stewart, isn't it?' His words stopped her breath again. He knew her son's name without being told. 'That was my father's name, as well.' He favoured the boy with the same harmless smile he had used on Ronald. But there was an ironic note in the statement that was hidden so deeply she could not be sure that it existed outside her imagination.

Stewart swallowed nervously. Then he smiled back and nodded.

Now the captain was touching her boy, taking him by the shoulders and turning him side to side to give him a thorough examination. She tensed, waiting for his reaction. 'You look very much like your mother.'

Was that meant to be ironic, as well? Or was it only she who noticed the way it focused attention on the lack of similarity between the boy and the Wiscombe family?

Why was he, of all people, not surprised to see this child? While the rest of the world might think it quite normal that she had a son, she must now face the one man in the world who would have questions.

And yet, he was not asking them. He was pretending to be simple and pleasant Gerald Wiscombe, and behaving as if he had expected this meeting all along. He had known the name of her boy because someone had told him. But who? How much had he been told? And how much of what he thought he knew was the actual truth of the situation?

Now he was questioning the boy in languages and receiving the sort of indifferent responses one could expect from a very young child who enjoyed the countryside more than the classroom.

When he had tried and failed to answer yet another simple question put to him in Latin, Stewart's limited patience evaporated. 'I am much better at mathematics than at Latin. Mama says that you are, too. Would you like to hear me do my sums?'

For the first time since he'd arrived, Captain Wiscombe's composure failed him. He might have known of Stewart's existence. But clearly he had not prepared himself to face a living, breathing child who was eager to give him the hero's welcome he deserved. His overly bright smile disappeared, as did the bitterness it hid. Stripped of his armour, she caught a glimpse of the awkward boy who had proposed to her, trapped in a social situation he was ill-equipped to manage.

Then the facade returned and he clapped the boy on the shoulder. 'Your sums. Well. Another time, perhaps. Now run along back to the schoolroom and leave the adults to their talk. I am sure you have a nurse or a governess about who is supposed to give you your dinner.'

Stewart hesitated, staring at the captain with a hunger that could not be filled by his dinner tray. But Wiscombe saw none of it, or at least pretended he did not. Now that he'd made his acknowledgement, his interest in the child had disappeared as quickly as it had arisen.

Her son shot a hopeful look in her direction, as if pleading on her part might earn him a reprieve.

She gave him a single warning shake of her head and a slight tilt of her chin towards the stairs. Captain Wiscombe was right. Until they had spoken in private, Stewart was better off taking tea in the nursery.

Once the boy was gone, her husband turned his attention to Ronald. 'I expect you have somewhere to be, as well.'

'Not really,' her brother replied with a bland smile. Now that he'd had time to recover from the shock of seeing Wiscombe, her brother's sangfroid had returned.

'Might I suggest you find somewhere?' Her husband was smiling, as well. But there was a glint in his eyes that promised mayhem if his orders were not obeyed immediately. Then he softened to harmlessness again and threw an arm around her, hauling her into his lap. 'After seven years away, it is not unreasonable that I wish to be alone with my wife.'

The sudden feeling of his arms tightening under her breasts and the rock-hard thighs beneath her bottom sucked the wind from her lungs and she was seeing spots again. *Breathe*, she reminded herself. *Just breathe.*

When she'd mastered her panic, she found her foolish brother was smiling in agreement as if he expected Captain Wiscombe was seeking immediate privacy so he might mount his wife in a common room. Could he not see that the gullible young man they'd roped into this union had returned as a dreadnought?

'Then I will leave the two of you alone,' Ronald said with a wink to Captain Wiscombe, treating her as though she were not even in the room with them. 'Do not worry, Lily. I will see to the dinner arrangements and tell the guests of the captain's arrival.' Then he disappeared, shutting the door behind him, totally unaware of the storm about to break when her husband gave vent to his true feelings.

'Yes, Ronald. Go and see to your guests. Inform them of my presence. I hope you remember to tell them enough about me so they can pretend that we share an acquaintance.' Now that he was gone, her husband made no effort to hide his scorn for her brother. She could feel his muscles tensing like a great cat gathering before the spring. Then he shifted, dumping her back out of his lap and on to the cushion at his side.

Lily moved as well, sliding to the far end of the small couch to put as much distance between them as possible. Never mind breathing, it was impossible to think when he was touching her. Even when he was not, she could feel an aura of virile energy emanating from him, raising the hairs on her skin.

Or perhaps he was simply angry. She rushed to fill the silence before the fear of him could suck the breath from her lungs again. 'If company is not to your liking, we will send them away immediately.'

'But that would be most rude,' he replied in a soft, mocking tone. 'And above all things, I would not want to be thought rude. Tell me, wife, who are my guests? I do not like being the last one to know what is going on in my own home.'

'Mr and Mrs Carstairs...' she began hesitantly.

'And they are...?' He made a coaxing gesture with his hand.

'A businessman from London, and his wife.'

'What is his trade?'

'I believe he is an ironmonger.'

'A wealthy one, I presume.'

She cleared her throat. 'I believe so.'

'Who else, then?'

'The Burkes and the Wilsons, also of London.'

'And also cits?'

'Yes, Captain.' How quickly she had fallen into the role of loyal subordinate. But there was something about the man that commanded respect, even in a private setting such as this one.

'Others?'

'Sir Chauncey d'Art and his friend, Miss Fellowes.' She hoped he did not wish her to speculate on the nature of the friendship. Though she had provided two rooms for the couple it was likely that only one of them was getting use.

'Is that all?'

'No, Captain.' She wet her lips. 'We are entertaining your neighbour, the Earl of Greywall.' He was the last person she wished her husband to meet. All the more reason that they should clear the house as quickly as possible.

'Greywall.' There was another moment of blank vulnerability before his smile returned and he counted on his fingers. 'If we add you, your father and brother, there are twelve.' The smile became a lopsided grin. 'Now that I am here, there shall be thirteen at dinner. I expect it will be quite unlucky for somebody.'

Lily threw caution to the winds and reached to

touch his arm, adding a smile warm enough to melt butter. If she used her imagination and all the talent she had inherited from Father, perhaps she might persuade him that she was glad to see him home and had not been dreading this moment for most of the time he'd been gone. 'Unlucky? Surely not. We are all fortunate to have you here.'

For a moment, it actually seemed to work. He softened and looked ready to cover her hand with his. Then he remembered that she was nothing more than a fraud and pulled away with a frustrated sigh. 'Really, madam. If you must lie to me, try not to be so transparent about it. The facts are these—your father and brother tricked me into marriage with you for their own ends and never intended for me to return. In giving me that commission, they thought they were sending me to my death. And you—'

'I'm sorry.' She blurted out the words before he could finish his sentence. 'Despite what you think of me, I am glad that you are safe.' She was relieved, at least. For years, she had been too afraid to pray for his return. But that was not the same as wishing him ill. Just as he had said in jest, she'd prayed for his safety each night.

'Are you?' His expression hardened. 'Then you are more foolish than I thought. After I am satisfied that you've paid for what they have done to me, I mean to put you and your family out in the street. The guests, as well. And your precious Stewart will be the first to go.'

She was feeling light-headed again, images impending of exile and humiliation swirling in her mind. But this time, she was not alone in her suffering. She had to be strong for Stewart. She took another deep breath and cast down her eyes to assure him she was beaten. 'It is within your right.'

He laughed. 'What? You are not going to plead for your safety? I would have thought, at least, you would have a word of defence for our darling boy. Are you not going to beg me? Tell me I am hard-hearted to turn the product of our love off the property he is heir to. Why, when I think of that one night of passion we shared...'

'Stop!' She could not bear his mocking a moment longer.

'Do you remember it differently?' he said, innocently. 'It has been so long. Perhaps I am mistaken. If so, tell me the truth of it now.'

She could not speak. Her tongue was frozen in her mouth, unwilling to speak the truth.

'Talk!'

If this was what he brought to the battlefield, it explained his success. His command was stronger than the fear that kept her silent. 'We shared no night,' she said, choking out the words. 'Only a brief ceremony, the breakfast and two separate rooms at the inn. We did not lie together. The next morning, you were gone.'

He nodded. 'I promised I would not come to you until we knew each other better. To be gone so soon and with no guarantee of a future…it did not seem fair to either of us.' For a moment, he sounded almost wistful for the innocents they had been.

Then his voice hardened. 'When I think of how it was, in those first months…I carried a miniature of you, everywhere I went. I kissed it each night at bed and before battles for luck. I was pure as a monk, waiting for the moment when I might come back to you. I wrote you dozens of letters. There was not a single response.'

She had been too upset to write. At first, she had been angry at him for being so foolish as to fall for the plan, going to what was likely certain doom. She was ashamed of herself as well, for obeying her father when she had known what they were doing was wrong. Later, she had been ashamed for other reasons and angry at him for leaving her alone and defenceless.

He did not notice her discomfiture and went on. 'When a commanding officer came to me, less than a year later, with the good news of the birth of my son?' He laughed at this, as though it were a ribald joke in a brothel. 'I did not have to feign surprise. We all went to a cantina, where I had to pay for the wine so they might drink my health, and to the health of my good wife and heir.'

He had known, almost from the first. It explained why his letters to her had stopped. 'When you stopped writing…I thought you had died.' Would he believe that she had cried over him? Probably not. But she had.

'That news was the making of my career,' he added. 'When a soldier has no reason to fear death, it leads to the sort of recklessness that makes heroes. Or corpses,' he added. 'I do not like to think of the men under my command who lacked the damnable luck of their leader.'

She'd felt bad enough knowing that he might lose his life because of Father's scheming. But to think that others had been affected and that she was in some way responsible for their fates made her guilt even heavier. 'I am sorry,' she said again.

'So you keep saying,' he said with a mocking smile. 'Tell me now. The truth, for once. Were you with child when we married? Was that the reason that your father rushed to unite us?'

'No!' There was much wrong between them, but she did not want to claim a fault that was not hers. Then she saw the change in his expression and knew that it would have been kinder had she lied.

'So you admit to cuckolding me.' He shook his head again. 'Were you really so sure I would die that you did not think I might return to see the consequences of your infidelity?'

The answer to that was very nearly yes. But it was so much more complicated than that. How could she even begin to explain? Having to talk

about it at all was bringing on one of her headaches. She rubbed her temple and tried to con-
centrate. 'At first, I did not know what to do. I
barely understood what was happening to me,
much less what to do about it. The longer I did
nothing, the easier it became to go on as I had
started.'

'How well does it work for you now?' he asked,
staring at her as though she had confirmed his
low opinion of her. 'And do not apologise to
me again. There is no apologising for what you
have done.'

There was an explanation. But it had been
years since that night. What proof could she
offer him that she spoke true? She took a breath
and squared her shoulders. 'At least the waiting
is finally over. You will do what you will do. I
do not have to imagine what that might be. My
only request—'

'You have no right to request anything of me.'
Once again, she heard the command in the voice
and understood how the boy she had married
had become a hero.

'I will do so, all the same. My son is not at

fault. If there is kindness in your heart at all, do not let the punishment fall on him.'

'You mean, on your bastard?'

She had been foolish to hope for better. 'My son,' she repeated softly. 'If you cannot mete out both shares of the punishment to me, then give me time to tell him the truth before he hears it from another.'

'He does not know?' For a moment, his anger was replaced by surprise.

'No one knows,' she said. 'A few people closest to me might guess. But no one is sure, other than you and me.'

'Not even...' He was wondering about Stewart's father.

He had been so drunk that night she doubted he even remembered what he had done. She shook her head. 'No one knows. And Stewart is far too young to understand. All his life, he has been fed on stories of the heroic father he has never met. To find that it is a lie... It will come as a shock.' This was not true. It would be utterly devastating to him.

'His heroic father,' the captain said with bitterness. 'And who is that man? I wish to congratulate him and make him aware of his responsibility. Or are your affairs so numerous that you cannot fix on a single name?'

She did not think he had the power to hurt her with mere words, but the question stung like a slap to the face. 'There was but one man and one night. I could point to it on a calendar, if you wish.' Not that she needed a paper record. The date and time, down to the minute, had been burned into her memory. The clock in the hall had been striking twelve as her life was ruined.

She shook her head, which was still ringing. 'I will not tell you his name. Nor will I tell Stewart. You are the only father he has ever known. He had been learning to read by following the news of your battles. His first toy was a wooden sword. He has entire battalions of tin soldiers and sets them to fighting each other at every opportunity. His only ambition is to grow to be as brave as you have been.'

'That is no doing of mine,' he insisted. But there was a gruffness in his voice that hinted at emotions other than anger. And then the brief flicker of sympathy vanished. 'You should not have lied to him.'

'Nor could I have told him the truth.' It was an awful enough story to carry on her own. She had no desire to taint the boy's life with it. 'I told him a partial truth at least. You are brave and worthy of his admiration. If he meant to create an idol, he could do much worse than you.'

'Do not think to flatter me,' the captain said. 'It will not work.'

But neither did it seem to be doing her any harm. This time, he had been the one to look away, as though her praise made him uncomfortable. 'It is not flattery if the statement is truth.'

'I didn't return to this house seeking your approval,' he snapped. The tenuous connection she'd created was gone. His gaze locked on hers again as his suspicion returned.

'I know that,' she said quickly. 'You owe me nothing and you need nothing from me.' But she could not believe it was in his nature to be cruel, even to an enemy. And certainly not to a child.

Suddenly, his look held speculation. 'On the contrary. I owe you much. I vowed before God to protect you. I do not like to break my word.' His voice did not sound kind. But neither was it as sharp as it had been.

Had she said something to change his mind? What had it been? She grasped at the opportunity. 'I made promises to you, as well,' she said, softly. 'And I have broken them. You deserved to find a virtuous wife waiting for your return. I failed you. I have failed Stewart, as well. If you could help me in any way...'

It had been too much to ask. He'd flinched at the mention of the boy's name.

She tried another way. 'If, once you have decided my fate, you could at least allow me enough time to speak to him, to try to tell him the truth gently, before...' Before they were turned out of the house, as he had threatened before. It was no less than she deserved. The only consolation she might find in it was that her brother and father would follow her in banishment. After seven years, this charade would finally be at an end.

Captain Wiscombe did not answer. He was staring at her in a way that made her even more nervous than before. His eyes held the same curious intensity that her father's sometimes did when he found a pigeon ripe for plucking.

Since she had no choice in the matter, she stood his scrutiny in mute embarrassment.

At last, he spoke. 'There is another possibility.'

She fought down the urge to agree without waiting for an explanation. Sometimes, she suspected she was far too obedient for her own good. It was quite possible that what he planned for her might be even worse than the humiliation she would experience when the truth about Stewart was revealed.

'You said I needed nothing from you.' His hand reached out to her, his fingers brushing her cheek. 'That is not precisely true.'

She could not help it. She shuddered. Part of it was nerves. But there was something else, something about the look in his eyes that raised other, more pleasant feelings in her. She was being touched by the dashing hero whose exploits she had followed for years. In person, he was even more handsome than she had imagined him. And he wanted her help. 'What do you wish from me?'

He smiled. 'What does any man wish from the woman he has married? Loyalty, my dear. Thus far, you have given me every reason to doubt that I have yours.'

Loyalty? That was disappointingly mundane. But it was also easily accomplished. According to *The Times*, Captain Gerald Wiscombe inspired devotion in all who knew him. She would much rather obey him than her less-than-honourable father. She dipped her head in consent. 'Despite appearances, you have my complete allegiance, sir. Let me prove it to you.'

'You will have to,' he said, 'if you wish to remain in the house even one more night.'

'Anything you want, I will get for you,' she said. 'What do you require?'

He was still looking at her with an intensity that sent chills down her spine. 'What do I want? Satisfaction. Reparation. Revenge. I have done my duty, in service of my king. I have seen things that no man should see and done things I would never have thought myself capable of. But I survived, madam. Though your father and brother thought they were sending me to my death, I survived. Now I mean to make them pay for what they have done. Are you with me, or against me?'

'With you, of course,' she replied without hesitation. Hadn't this been exactly what she had longed for? Someone to come and make her family regret its selfishness? It would be her pleasure to help him.

'You answered very quickly. It is as if you didn't think about it at all.' He nodded in mocking approval. 'Do you expect me to believe you without question?'

'You are my husband,' she said. 'By the laws of man and church, I must answer to you in all things. My father and brother have no say in the matter.'

'Just as you no longer have a say in what will happen to my son,' he said, with a wicked smile. 'The fact that you bore him does not give you the right to decide his future. You are but a woman and I am the head of the house.'

'Your son?' Her heart stuttered eagerly. Did he mean to claim the boy?

'You have declared him so,' the captain reminded her. 'If you did not wish me to have power over him, you should have told the truth.'

'What do you mean to do with him?' she said, suddenly afraid.

He fixed her with an insincere smile. 'If you do as I say? Nothing so terrible. When we have cleared this house of your family and their accompanying friends, I will find a school for the boy. He will start as soon as it can be arranged and will remain there over summer and for holidays as well. He will be perfectly safe, fed, clothed and cared for. But he will no longer live in my house, pretending to be my blood. Until the time comes for him to go, you will keep him out of my sight. I do not wish to be reminded of his presence.'

She had known that school was in Stewart's future, but not for a few years, at least. He was still so young. This was not education, it was banishment. Stewart would be crushed when he realised that the father he worshipped could not bear the sight of him. And when he was gone, she would lose the only unsullied love she had ever known.

He had noticed her silence. 'It will not be so different from my own childhood,' he said, with a shrug. 'My father sent me to Eton when I was eight. I stayed between terms when he was away from the house. I grew to prefer it to home.'

'Stewart is much younger than that,' she said in a whisper.

He gave her a pitying look. 'Surely you did not expect that we would remain together as a happy family.'

'Of course not,' she lied. But he was the hero of Salamanca. She had been hoping for a miracle.

'Well, then you understand that I am being more generous than most men in this position.'

She nodded, for it was true. But she did not care. She needed more than this. Boarding school was an improvement over the immediate exile he had been threatening less than an hour ago. If he was given time to get to know the boy, she must trust that his mood would soften even more.

'Will you stand with me, or against me?' he said.

'With you, of course,' she said, eager for the chance to prove her worth to him. 'I am yours to command.'

'Very good,' he said with a nod. 'I am glad we have an understanding.'

He stood and walked towards the door. Then

he stopped and turned back to her again, placing his index finger against his chin as though there was some point they had forgotten to discuss. Then he smiled, as if the idea had suddenly come back to him. 'We have not yet discussed what is to become of you, after all is settled.'

'Me?' The word came out in a squeak, like a mouse that had just been caught in a trap.

'There is more to being a wife then parroting "yes" each time I ask a question. I expect you to share my bed, as well.' He'd added it in an offhand manner, as though it was a minor consideration, hardly worth mentioning. 'You will submit to me whenever I request it. I will use you as I please, when I please. If I tire of you, I will abide no fussing or tears. Under no circumstances will you be taking admirers of your own. I said I wanted loyalty, my dear, and in the bedroom it will be absolute.'

His eyes narrowed in satisfaction at her look of shock. 'The alternative is that I turn you from the house this very day. There will be no time for niceties. You will leave with your whelp and the clothes on your back, and the devil take you both.'

The fear of that was clearer and more immediate than anything that might happen in the captain's bed. She gave a hesitant nod.

He nodded back at her, the old, harmless smile returning. 'Very good. I knew we could come to an understanding, if we had a few moments alone to talk.'

She fought against another shiver. If she thought about it, she would realise that this meeting had gone better than she could have hoped. Stewart would be safe. She would be rid of her family. And as long as he had a use for her, she might keep her place as lady of the house. It was not the stuff of fairy tales, but it never had been.

More importantly, this was Gerald Wiscombe ordering her to his bed. If she searched, she might still find traces of the gentle, awkward boy who had postponed the consummation of their marriage to spare her feelings. At the very least, he was an officer and a gentleman, not some uncaring brute. If she did what he asked of her, he would not hurt her just for the sport of seeing her suffer.

He was also the hero of Salamanca.

Half the women in England swooned at the

mention of his name. In their midnight fantasies, they offered themselves to the gallant and heroic Captain Wiscombe, thanking him for his service with their bodies.

Would it surprise him to discover that his wife was no different? That she felt a dark thrill at his command to submit to his desires? If he had meant it as a punishment, he would be just as likely to reject her again, should she seem too eager for his attention.

She stood so that she might look him in the eye and pretend that it did not matter to her if he wanted her or not.

Then, as if to prove just how false her bravery was, he pulled her forward into his arms and kissed her hard upon the lips.

It was over just as quickly. But fantasy paled in comparison. He had told her with a single kiss that he was her lord and master and she had responded as if she longed to be ruled by him. When he released her, she fell back into the cushions of the divan, weak from the sudden loss of control over her body and her future. Before she could comment, he rose, walked out of the room and left her alone.

Chapter Four

In Belgium, when they'd all thought the war was over, there had been far too much time to drink and reminisce with other officers. Gerry had noticed a certain arrogance on the part of the infantry commanders towards their counterparts in the cavalry. Given any excuse, they would insist that fighting from horseback was not real fighting at all.

To be above the action and looking down upon it was, in their opinion, to cheat. Not only did it give the rider a tactical advantage, but it removed the need to face the enemy eye to eye. Bravery, to an infantryman, was to see all of the common thoughts and emotions that rendered one man equal to another reflected in an enemy's face, and to attack in spite of them.

Today he wondered if there might be truth in that. When he'd imagined himself coming home, it had been in a metaphorical galloping charge. It would be the work of an instant to vanquish the interlopers who had claimed his home. He would take special pleasure in seeing his wife wailing and gnashing her teeth as he put her out and slammed the door in her face.

In his imagination, it was always raining the kind of cold drizzle that one got in the north. It added an extra air of pitifulness to her entreaties and those of the rat-faced whelp clinging to her skirts.

The actual meeting had been quite different. Evidence still proved she was a cheating whore. But he'd thought she would make some effort to deny the obvious. Perhaps she would try to hide the child. At the very least, she would have some tragic story to explain it.

Instead, she had offered complete surrender before he could strike a metaphorical blow. Even worse, she had displayed her greatest weakness. She wished to protect her son even if it meant sacrificing herself. She had not even resorted to the weapon all women seemed to use against men. Not a single tear had been shed as she'd awaited his judgement.

These were not the actions of a worthy opponent. She was behaving like a martyr. Even worse, the boy showed no mark of his mother's perfidy. Because of Lillian's lies, the child seemed illogically eager to see him. To send him away would be like kicking a puppy because it had wagged its tail.

After the interview, he'd felt dirtied by more than the grime of travel. There was no fault in expecting fidelity and no villainy in being angry when one did not receive it. There was no sin in demanding that one's wife behave like a wife, in bed and out, if she wished to remain under one's roof. But if all that was true, then why did staring into those sad brown eyes make him feel like a lecherous cad?

And what had the kiss meant to either of them? Compared to his plans to take her to bed, it had seemed almost chaste. But at the end of it, she had been shaking in his arms and he had been left unsettled, ready to saddle his horse and go before closer contact with her made him forget her unfaithfulness.

He would feel better after a drink and a wash. But apparently, that was too much to ask. 'Aston! Mrs Fitz!' He roared for the servants in his best battlefield voice and was satisfied to hear doors opening and closing up and down the guest-room corridors. His unwanted visitors had learned the master of the house was home and was not happy.

The servants appeared, out of breath and in unison, before he had to call a second time.

He pointed to the door to his room. 'What is the meaning of this?' There was a shiny brass lock on the door of the master bedroom, where none had been before.

'Oh. Oh, sir. I mean, Captain, I am so sorry.' His poor housekeeper was devastated that their first meeting after his return was because of an error in her management. 'When the maid aired the room and lit the fire, she locked it after. It is always locked. The mistress's room, as well.'

'I see that.' He had tried the door just down the hall from his, thinking he could enter his own room through the connecting door. He had been blocked there, as well. 'Am I expected to break down the benighted doors to gain admittance, then?'

'No, sir.' Aston was fishing on his ring for a key. He turned it in the lock and then placed it in his master's hand. Gerry's single glance down the hall to his wife's room had the servant relinquishing that key as well.

'We meant no insult by it,' Mrs Fitz said hurriedly.

'Of course you did not. But what is the purpose of such security?'

Aston cleared his throat. 'There are frequent guests here. Strangers to the house sometimes wander down the wrong hallway and disturb the peace. Mrs Wiscombe thought it better that the family rooms be locked when not in use.'

'Yours especially, Captain Wiscombe,' Mrs Fitz said, as though it was somehow a point of pride. 'She was adamant that no matter how full the house, your room was to be kept empty and ready for your return.'

'As it should be,' he said. The housekeeper gave his wife far too much credit for simple common sense. 'Before I left, I gave the Norths permission to use the house as their own. But it is not as if we are running some roadside hostel with rooms to let.'

There was an uncomfortable silence from the two servants at his side.

'I said, my home is not an inn.' His voice was rising again, as was his temper.

Aston cringed. 'Of course not, Captain Wiscombe.' Then why did he sound doubtful?

'But?' Gerry gave a coaxing twitch of his fingers and waited for the rest of the story.

'The Misters North entertain here. Frequently,' Mrs Fitz said, with a little sniff of disapproval.

'There are often large house parties,' Aston supplied. 'Guests come from the city for hunting and cards.'

'Friends of the family?' Gerry suggested.

'The Earl of Greywall is usually among the party. But the rest...' Aston looked uncomfortable. 'Very few guests are invited twice.'

'I see.' In truth, he did not. Why would Ronald and his father bring crowds of strangers to such a remote location? And why was Greywall here? He knew he was not welcome and he had a perfectly good residence only a few miles away.

He considered. 'Is the earl in residence now?'

'Yes, sir.'

Damn. When he was alive, Gerry's father had loathed the peer who could not seem to limit himself to the game on his own side of the property line. After he'd died, Greywall had not waited for the body to cool before he'd begun to pester Gerry to sell house and land for less than they were worth. The crass insensitivity of his offers had convinced Gerry that anything, including a sudden marriage and military career, would be preferable to giving in to Greywall's demands.

His stubbornness had netted nothing if the earl had caged a permanent invitation to house and grounds. It was about to be rescinded, of course. But it would have to be done carefully. Even peers one did not like demanded special handling in situations like this. He sighed. 'Then I suspect I will meet him and the rest over dinner.'

'Very good, sir. Do you require assistance in changing? A shave, perhaps?'

'As long as my bag and kit are waiting, I can manage on my own,' he said, although the thought of the master dressing without help clearly appalled his poor butler. He gave them both an encouraging smile. No matter what had occurred in his absence, the staff was not at fault. 'It is good to be home,' he added.

They smiled back, and Mrs Fitz bobbed a curtsy. 'And to see you again, safe and well, sir. If you need anything...'

'I will ring,' he assured her and gave a brief nod of thanks to dismiss them. Then he opened the door and entered his room.

For a moment, he paused on the threshold, confused. Before his sudden marriage and equally sudden departure, he'd never felt at home in the master suite. He had gone from the nursery to school, returning only on news of his father's death. For most of his life this had not been his space at all, but his father's.

He'd felt woefully out of place during the few months he'd been master of the house. Days had been spent in his father's study trying to decipher the bookkeeping and poring over stacks of unpaid bills. Nights had been marked with uneasy sleep in his father's bed, too embarrassed to admit that he missed his cot in the nursery. How was one expected to get any rest, surrounded by so many judgemental eyes?

His father had been a mediocre parent, but an avid sportsman. The bedroom, like so many other rooms in the house, was full of his trophies. Gerry did not mind the pelts, so much. He would even admit to a childish fascination for the rugs of tiger and bearskin in the billiard room. But what was the point of decorating the room in which one slept with the heads of animals one had killed? Stags stared moodily down from the walls. Foxes sat on the mantel, watching him with beady glass eyes. Antlers and boar tusks jutted from the wall behind the bed as though they might, at any moment, fall to impale the sleeper.

Gerry had proved in countless battles that he was no coward. When the killing was done, he'd treated the dead with as much respect as he was able. He had hoped for the same, should his luck fail him and circumstances be reversed. A gentleman should not gloat on the lives he'd taken, especially not at bedtime.

His father had not shared the sentiment. Of course, to the best of Gerry's knowledge, his father had never killed a man, much less dozens of them. The stuffed heads had been nothing more than decorations to him. But to Gerry, they would be reminders of other soulless eyes, judging him as he tried to sleep. It was with trepidation that he opened the door tonight, prepared for the distasteful sights within.

He stood on the threshold, confused.

Today, as he'd walked through the house, he'd noted the subtle changes that had been made to the decorating. The overt masculinity had been retained. There could be no doubt that he was in a hunting lodge and not a London town house. But the stained and faded silks had been removed from the walls and replaced. Paint had been freshened. Furniture had been re-upholstered and rearranged. Though most of the trophies remained where he remembered them, they had at least been dusted. One could entertain both ladies and gentlemen here, without fear of embarrassment.

But no room he'd seen so far had been so totally transformed as his own bedroom. The dusty velvet chairs had been replaced with benches and stools covered in saddle leather. The heavy green baize on the walls had been exchanged for a cream-coloured, watered silk. The hangings over the bed were no longer maroon brocade. They were now a blue sarsenet shot through with silver. To stare up at the canopy would be like staring into a night sky full of stars.

The table at the side of the bed held the two volumes of the *Théorie Analytique des Probabilités* and a fine wooden version of Roget's new slide rule. He'd heard about the advances in mathematics since he'd been away and had been eager to return to his books. If he wished, he could take up his studies this very night.

Best of all, he could do it without the distractions of dozens of glass eyes. All evidence of his father's skill as a hunter had been removed. The walls were decorated with watercolour landscapes. He stepped closer to admire the work and started in surprise.

He knew the place in the picture. He had been there himself. It was Talavera de la Reina in Spain. But the picture was of the sleepy village and not the backdrop for battle. The next was of the Nive flowing through France. And here was Waterloo. Beautiful places all, not that he'd had the time to enjoy the scenery when he was there. But this was how he wanted to think of them. The land had healed. The blood he had shed was not muddying the dust. It had soaked into the ground and left only grass and wild-flowers as memorial to the dead.

As he admired the work, he felt relaxed and at peace, as though he had finally come home. This was *his* room, totally and completely. If he had written his wishes out and sent them ahead, he could not have been more pleased with the re-sults. The years of sacrifice had been rewarded with a haven of tranquillity. He could leave the war behind and become the man he had once intended to be.

This must have been Lillian's doing. No mere servant would have dared to take such liberties. Hadn't Mrs Fitz said it had been his wife's orders to keep the place locked until his return? But how had she known what he would like? How had she managed this without consulting him?

Most importantly, why had she done it?

Chapter Five

'The diamonds, or the pearls, madam?' The maid was holding one earring to each ear, so Lily could judge the effect in her dressing table mirror.

She frowned back at her own reflection. She wished to look her best for the captain's first night at home. Despite their current difficulties, she could not help the wistful desire that he might admire her looks and perhaps even comment on them. When he'd proposed she had been a foolish young girl, so supremely confident in her ability to enthral him that she hadn't even bothered to try. She certainly wouldn't have needed jewels to enhance her appearance. But now that he could compare her to half the señoritas and mademoiselles of Europe she was obsessing over each detail in an effort to win his praise.

And what message did it send to wear jewellery that he had not bought for her? The diamonds had been a gift from Father for her last birthday. But suppose he suspected they'd come from a lover? It would be better to wear the pearls she'd inherited from her mother. She'd been wearing them on the day the captain had proposed.

Would he remember them? Even if he did not, they were modest enough that he could not accuse her of profligate spending or accepting gifts from strangers. She pointed to the pearl drops and the maid affixed them and brought out the matching necklace.

On her left hand, she wore the simple gold ring that had belonged to his mother. When they'd married, he'd had nothing else to offer her but the ring and the house. His fortunes had improved since then. She was not sure how much money he had sent back from Portugal, but his banker in London had assured her that any bills she submitted would be paid without question. She hoped he was a rich man. He deserved to live comfortably after sacrificing a third of his life to the army.

But she had done nothing to earn a share of his wealth and had done her best not to abuse his generosity. She had taken very little from the accounts for frivolities, preferring to make sparing use of the allowance that had been provided for her. One of the first lessons learned as a member of the North family was to keep back a portion of any success for the moment when things went wrong and a quick escape was necessary. To that end, she had a tightly rolled pile of bank notes hidden in her dresser that not even her father was aware of.

The gown she was wearing had been one of her rare purchases, a London design that had arrived not two weeks ago. The pearls did not suit it at all, but they would have to do.

There was a knock on the bedroom door and her brother entered without waiting for her welcome.

She did not bother to turn to him, frowning at his reflection. 'Such rude behaviour is why my door is almost always locked.'

'Surely you have nothing to worry about, with

your husband in the next room.' Ronald was smiling back at her, as if he thought the prospect of rescue was unlikely, even if she needed it.

'You have more to fear from Captain Wiscombe than I do,' she said, amazed that he would joke about such a thing.

'The day will never come when I can't out-think Gerry Wiscombe.' Ronald's arrogance was undimmed by recent events. 'Nothing he said to you today after I left the room will make me believe otherwise.'

This was probably his way of requesting a report of her conversation with the captain. She ignored it, turning her attention back to her maid so that they might finish her toilette.

Ronald made no move to leave her, leaning against the wall by the door and staring as she made Jenny re-pin her braids and fuss over the ribbons at her shoulders until it was plain to everyone in the room that she was stalling. At last, she gave up and dismissed the maid, remaining silent until the door was shut and she could hear the girl's retreating footsteps at the far end of the hall.

'Well?' her brother said, arms folded over his chest. 'What did he say to you?'

She stared back at him, expressionless. 'If the words were meant for you, he'd have spoken them in your presence.'

'Ho-ho,' Ronald responded with an ugly smirk. 'You mean to side with him in this?'

She blinked innocently. 'Was that not the intention, when you and Father gave me to him?'

'I doubt Father expected that the day would come when you would throw your own flesh and blood to the wolves to save yourself.'

'Throw you to the wolves?' She laughed. 'If Captain Wiscombe has a problem with you or Father, I will have no say in it.'

'But what about your son?'

'What of him?' she said. Ronald had always been the least subtle of the Norths, trying to force information from her rather than waiting for it to be revealed. She turned back to the mirror, giving full attention to her appearance and none to his simmering anger.

'Gerry did not seem overly surprised by his presence.'

'Why should he be? We are married. There is

a child.' Ronald had hinted his suspicions before. Now was not the time to confirm them.

'Your child was born nearly ten months after your husband left for the army.'

'You exaggerate,' she said, adding a touch more powder to her cheeks. She shouldn't have bothered. The addition took her from perfection to unhealthy pallor.

'When Stewart's next birthday arrives, even a man as stupid as Gerry Wiscombe will count out the months and have questions for you.'

She turned to glare at him. 'My husband is no fool.'

At this, her brother laughed out loud. 'So sorry to offend you, little sister. If that is what you wish, I will try not to think of him as the poor gull who I tricked into marrying you.'

'You tricked him?' Now she was the one who doubted.

'I told him you had seen him from afar. That it was practically a love match and that all it would take to win one of the most celebrated beauties of the Season was a show of courage on his part and an offer. He asked for your hand.

Then, dutifully as a child, he ran off to war to impress you.'

'That is how you remember it?' Perhaps Gerald had shown a different face to her family than he had to her. Though his proposal had been gallant enough, she'd got no sense that he was dazzled by her beauty. He'd been a man with a plan. Marriage to her had been little more than a point of intersection between his goals and those of her father.

Her brother was still smiling at the memory. 'I had never met a fellow so easily persuaded or so quick to act against his own best interests as Gerry Wiscombe the day he proposed to you. It was a pity he had nothing more to offer than the house. If there had been money in his purse, I'd have got it all in one hand of cards.'

'It does not matter who he was when he left England,' Lily said, disgusted. 'The man who returned is different from the boy you remember.'

'So you claim,' he said with a sceptical nod. 'But when we spoke today he was the same amiable dolt I went to school with.'

'His successes on the Peninsula were not those

of a halfwit. If you'd read the accounts of the battles...'

Ronald held up a hand to stop her. 'Your obsession with the war has always been most unladylike. Now that Napoleon is imprisoned, I wish to hear no more of it. Even your brave captain admitted that it was luck that saw him safely home. That seems far more likely than a magical transformation into a man of action. Just an hour ago, he was smiling over nothing and all but upsetting your wine glass.'

'It is an act,' she said and immediately wondered if she had already broken her vow of loyalty to her husband by giving him away. But his bravery and tactical acumen were hardly a secret to one who bothered to read the papers. 'Even if he was not shamming this afternoon, you must realise that he plans to take control of his estate. Your games with Father must end.'

'Must they?' Ronald gave her an innocent stare. 'I see no reason that they cannot continue, once we have taken the time to convince Gerry of their usefulness.'

'You mean to convince a man of honour to run what is little more than a crooked gaming hell?'

Her brother clucked his tongue at her. 'Such a way to describe your own home. This is not a professional establishment. It is merely a resort for those from the city who like sport, good wine and deep play.'

'Call it what you will,' she said. 'It is not, and never has been, your house. Now that the master has returned, things will be different.'

'Yes, they will,' Ronald agreed. 'Once Gerry has settled his account with us...'

'Settled with you?'

'The upkeep on such a large place is extensive. The slates. The curtains. The wine in the cellar...'

'You do not mean to charge him for wine that he has not even tasted. And though he gave you permission to live here, he did not ask you to fix up the house.'

Ronald held his hands palms up in an innocent shrug. 'I am sure he did not intend for us to live with rain pouring through the holes in the roof. Something needed to be done. How much blunt does he have, do you think?'

'Even if I knew, I would not tell you.' However much he had, her brother would see to it that the captain owed him double. If a direct appeal for funds failed, Ronald would win it at cards or billiards, or through any other weakness that could be discovered and exploited. Before he knew it, her husband would have empty pockets and the struggles of the past few years would be for naught. That was the way the Norths did business.

Ronald smiled. 'We might be persuaded to forget his debt, as we did for Greywall. The chance to meet the famous Captain Wiscombe will bring even more people up from London. I am sure he must have friends recently retired from service who would enjoy a chance to share our hospitality. We simply have to persuade him.'

'You will never convince him to do such a thing,' she said, praying that it was true.

'Perhaps not. But I will not have to. You are so very good with men, little sister,' he said, touching her shoulder.

She shrugged off his hand. 'I will not help you hurt him.'

'You did once, Lillian.' He patted her shoulder again.

'And I regret it,' she said. She had been young

and foolish, and there had been no choice. It would not happen again.

'Regret?' Ronald laughed. 'You are a North, Lillian. That is not an emotion we are capable of. The time will come when blood will tell and you will come around to our way of thinking again.'

'Never,' she said.

'We shall see. But now I must go to my own room to dress. I will see you at dinner.' He smiled. 'Remember to look your best for Gerry. If he is a happy and contented husband, it will be that much easier to bring him into the fold. And once we are assured of his help, we will be even better off than before.'

As it usually was at Wiscombe Chase, dinner was a motley affair. Guests were either tired from the hunt, well on the way to inebriation, or both. Today, most of them still wore their fox-hunting pinks, having gone from the stable to the brandy decanter without bothering to change for dinner.

At the centre of the table, as it so often was, there was venison. When she'd first arrived here, Lily had liked the meat. She had to admit that

Cook prepared it well. The haunch was crisp at the end and rare and tender in the middle. The ragout was savoury, with thick chunks of vegetables from the kitchen garden. The pies were surrounded by a crust that flaked and melted in the mouth like butter.

But venison today meant that yesterday another stag had been shot and butchered. The supply of them seemed endless, as did the stream of guests that came to hunt them. Was it too much to ask that, just once, a hunt would end in failure? Perhaps then the word would spread that the Chase was no longer a prime destination to slaughter God's creatures.

Of course, if there were no more deer, they would just switch to quail. A brace of them had been served in aspic as the first course. At tomorrow's breakfast, there would be Stewart's fresh fish. A starving person might have praised the Lord for such abundance, but Lily had come to dread meals when requesting vegetables had begun to feel like an act of defiance.

At the head of the table, Captain Wiscombe stared down the length at the plates and gave a single nod of approval. His eye turned to the guests and the approbation vanished. And then he looked at her. Did she see the slightest scornful curl of his lip?

He must think her totally without manners to have arranged the table with no thought to precedence. But she could hardly be blamed for the tangled mess that these dinners had become. Attempts to arrange the ladies according to rank before entry to the dining room were met with failure, as none of them seemed to understand their place. If she resorted to name cards beside their plates, they simply rearranged them and sat according to who wished to speak to whom. The men were even worse, with businessmen bullying lords to take the place next to the earl.

With the addition of Captain Wiscombe, things were even more out of balance than usual. The ladies at either side of him were the youngest of the four. Miss Fellowes, who had pulled her chair so close that she was brushing his right sleeve with her arm, was not even married. Mrs Carstairs hung on his left, laughing too loudly at everything that he said, as though polite dinner conversation were a music-hall comedy.

Her father and brother had packed themselves

into the middle of the table on either side and chatted animatedly with the guests who lacked the spirit to fight for a better chair.

On her end of the table, the earl took her right, as he always did. He remained oblivious to the insult of the cit at his other side, as long as he was supplied with plenty of wine and an opportunity to ogle her décolletage.

The space between them was punctuated by silence. He had long ago learned that if he attempted to speak to her, she would not respond. But even if she did not look in his direction, she could still feel his eyes upon her like a snail trail on her skin. She took a deep sip of her wine to combat the headache that came with pretending indifference to it.

On her left was Sir Chauncey, staring dejectedly up the table at Miss Fellowes as though watching his romantic hopes disappearing over the horizon. Tonight she made a half-hearted effort to engage him in conversation, to take his mind from the sight of his lover flirting with her husband. But eventually she tired of his monosyllabic responses and let their end of the table return to silence.

Then she looked towards the head of the table as well and hoped that the captain would not catch her studying him. Who would have thought that a shy boy could turn into such a magnificent creature? Even when at ease, he still had the air of command that she had noticed in the sitting room earlier. He did not stare, nor did his eyes dart from face to face. Yet he seemed aware of each action taken and each word spoken up and down the table.

While he took care that this observation of his guests did not seem ill-mannered, the women surrounding him did not bother with niceties. They stared openly at the way the candlelight shone gold off the waves in his hair and the shadows accented the sharp planes of his cheeks. When he smiled, and he did so often, they could not contain audible sighs of admiration. Fox hunting might have held their attention this afternoon. But if such a fine male specimen showed even a hint of interest, the women of the party would be doing any future sporting inside the house with the captain.

The feeling this aroused in her was unfamiliar, but she assumed it must be jealousy. It explained the urge she had to pry the two women away from him and claim the place at his side. When she'd imagined his homecoming, it had not been at all like this.

For one thing, he was even more splendid to look at then she'd dreamed. She had pictured him as growing taller, leaner and more mature, an older version of the ordinary boy who had left her. She had not expected the blond god lounging at the head of the table tonight.

She stared, fascinated, as he rolled the stem of his wine glass between his fingers. Was it a sign of irritation? Boredom? Or was it simply a habit? It did not matter what it meant to him. To her, it hinted that the hands that had been brutal on the battlefield were gentle enough to hold a wine glass, or a woman.

Miss Fellowes was watching his hands, as well. And there was another difference. In Lily's fantasies, there had been no competition for his attention. Nor had he stated plainly, during their first conversation, that he might desire others and that she was to have no say in the matter.

She should have spent less time on dreams and focused on the harsh realities. He had no reason to like her, much less love her. Even in the best marriages, male fidelity was not guaranteed or expected.

Her father had no such trepidations. He was smiling up the table as if Christmas had arrived in September. A dragoon in dress uniform was just what the table needed to convince a band of foolish cits that they were dining with the upper class. The splendid red jacket hugging his shoulders had an excessive amount of gold braid covering it. Despite the time spent on horseback, the breeches beneath it were still snowy white and tight enough to display the muscles of a superlative horseman. Though the captain's excuse was that his clothing would arrive in a day or two, the full uniform made him into just the sort of prize that would have guests swarming to the Chase to meet him.

Her father stood, raising his glass. 'May I offer a toast to our host and thanks for his safe return?'

Lily tried to contain her flinch. No, he might not. If a toast was to be made, especially so early in the meal, her husband should be the one to offer it. Even while attempting courtesy, her father was rudely overstepping his place.

Gerald accepted it with a smile and only the slightest narrowing of his eyes, to show his annoyance.

As she feared they would, the guests responded not with a polite, 'Hear, hear', but with raucous laughter and applause. The toast itself resulted in several spills on the linen and a cracked glass from Mr Wilson. Greywall, who always drank twice as much as the other guests, needed to have his glass refilled before he could participate. He drained it rather than sipping and gestured for the footman to leave the bottle. He turned to smile at her, lifting his glass in a private salute, and Lily could feel the slight pain in her head turning to a full megrim, tightening about her temples like an iron band.

From halfway down the table, Mr Burke began to regale them with a tale of the day's hunt. Conversation on all sides ground to a halt, except for the interjection of needless details by Mr Wilson and a brief argument between the two over whether the wind was easterly or from the west when the dogs first caught the scent.

At the head of the table, her husband was silent. His eyes were on his guests, but the knife in his hand was slicing the meat on his plate with mathematical precision.

When, at last, the poor vixen had been run to ground and her gory dispatch applauded, the table turned to Captain Wiscombe for his reaction.

He responded with a smile. Then, very deliberately, he set down his knife and fork and pushed his plate of venison away as if he'd lost all appetite.

Mr Burke stared at him in surprise. 'Do not tell me, Captain, that you do not enjoy hunting.'

'Not so much that I would wish to kill the animal a second time, during the meal,' he said, continuing to smile.

'Surely a little blood does not bother you, Wiscombe,' Greywall said. He forked up a large bite of rare meat and waved it before him as if to goad his host.

'A little blood?' He considered for a moment. 'It depends on whom it belongs to. I am more bothered by a small amount of mine than a large amount of another fellow's. And that of a fox?' He shrugged. 'If it does not come into my home to provoke me, then I see no reason to run through its home with a pack of dogs, waving my gun.'

'Did you see very much blood, when you were in Portugal?' This question came from Mrs Carstairs, who seemed to find nothing unlady-like in broaching such a topic at the table.

The others at the table leaned in expectantly.

Lily held her breath.

'See blood? Yes. Yes, I did. But, unlike a fox hunter, I did not intentionally rub it on my face to mark my first kill.' His smile dimmed and his distant expression made her wonder if he still saw carnage when he closed his eyes at night.

Mrs Carstairs was as oblivious to the slight as she was to the small fleck of blood left on her cheek from her first hunt. 'I am sure you have stories that are far more interesting than Mr Burke's. Was stalking Napoleon and his men so different from hunting dumb beasts?'

He thought for a moment. 'I wonder if, in a table somewhere in France, there is a man being asked the same thing about hunting me?' He offered nothing more than that, staring at her with a fixed smile until she looked away and changed the subject.

* * *

When dinner had ended, her father stopped her before she could escape to her room to ease the pain in her head. 'Lillian, a moment, please.'

For a moment, she considered pretending she had not heard him, as she usually did when he spoke to her. She had learned, years ago, that there was little point in conversing if she could not believe anything he might say. But if they did not talk here, he would follow her to her room, just as Ronald had done. A conversation in the hallway would be shorter and less painful. She rubbed her temple. 'What do you want?'

'I have not yet got the chance to speak to your husband about the future of our endeavours here. And I was wondering if you—'

She cut him off. 'It will not be necessary. There is no future for them.' Then she glanced about her to remind him that they were on the main floor where anyone might overhear them.

'No future?' He seemed surprised. 'It has taken years to get things running just as they are. We cannot stop now.'

'On the contrary. What you are doing is wrong. You should stop it immediately.'

Her father was looking at her as Stewart had, when she'd explained that nice little boys did not pull Kitty's tail. 'Wrong? The guests enjoy their visits here. In fact, they leave as happy as they arrive.'

'But poorer,' she reminded him.

'But they do not mind it,' he argued. 'If they do not, then I fail to see why you do.'

'The fact that they do not mind it does not make it right,' she said. She was using her patient, mothering voice. But she did not feel at all patient. She should not have to teach decency to this man. He should have been the one who taught it to her. The imaginary metal band that circled her head was tightening with each word.

'Right and wrong are nebulous things, Lillian. If no one is hurt, has a wrong truly been done?'

'How would you know that no one has been hurt?' she snapped. 'Have you ever asked them? Have you thought, for even a moment, about anyone other than yourself?' She was getting angry. If she was not careful, people would notice. And then everything would be worse and not better. She took several slow, deep breaths and felt the pain in her head lessen somewhat.

Other than to stare at her in shocked silence, her father did nothing. And that was just as expected.

When she'd calmed herself enough to continue, she said, 'What happens will be Captain Wiscombe's decision, because it is his house. He is an honourable man and he will want no part in the humbug you have created.'

Her father favoured her with a childishly eager smile. 'Then you must make an effort to persuade him.'

'I?' she said, shaking her head in amazement at his stubbornness. 'After all that has happened in this house, you come to me for help to keep things as they are?'

Now his expression turned to one of puzzlement. 'Of course I do. Who else could better help me persuade the captain?'

The pain in her head was near to unbearable. If she did not go to her room soon, the servants would have to carry her there. 'Even if I wanted to help you, what makes you think he would listen to me?'

Now it was her father's turn to speak to her as

if she were an ignorant child. 'Because he dotes on you, my dear.'

'He certainly does not.' If anything, the opposite was true. She'd had years to develop an infatuation with her own husband. But his affection grew more unattainable with each passing minute. 'He hates me,' she said and the ache in her head seemed to move to her heart.

'Nonsense. He adored you when he offered. I saw the look in his eyes after you'd accepted him. It was as if the crown jewels had fallen out of a tree and landed in his lap. I am sure nothing has changed.'

He was telling her what she wanted to hear, to win her to her side. But then, her father had always been good at making people believe in the impossible, even as he ignored the obvious. She must not be swayed by him. 'Everything has changed, Father. *Everything.*'

He smiled. 'Then you must change them back. Captain Wiscombe might have prevailed against Napoleon's army. But you, Lillian, are a North. The poor man does not stand a chance.'

Chapter Six

Gerry had begun to envy his wife her megrim.

Lillian had claimed illness and disappeared immediately after the meal, forcing the female guests to settle in the parlour with only a footman for company. The elder North and the earl had joined them, seeking a quiet game of cards by the fire.

The other men were proving themselves to be as annoying after dinner as they had been at the table. At Ronald's suggestion, the six of them remaining had retired with their port to the billiard room.

Either Lillian had not completed her redecorating, or she had given up on trying to make this room look like anything other than what it was. The tiny game room retained the utter lack of charm that had been so evident in the home of his youth. Hunting trophies still lined its upper walls, staring down at them as they played. Their glassy eyes glittered in the smoke from too many pipes and cigars.

Gerry leaned against the wall under a moth-eaten roe, sipping a brandy and watching as Lillian's brother toyed with his third opponent of the night. It was clear from the way he played that no one had bothered to take care of the slight warp that existed in the surface of the table, nor had they taken the time to properly iron the baize covering before the game began. The small wrinkles that still marred its surface would make play difficult.

The problems were near invisible to the naked eye, especially in a smoky room. But Gerry had found his ball trapped by the table's deficiencies often enough when learning the game from a competitive father who showed no mercy. When he'd whined about the unfairness of it, his father announced that a man who played a game without assessing the risks deserved what he got.

The elder Wiscombe would have got along well with the Norths. Tonight, Ronald was using the same philosophy to remove money from his guests. Poor Carstairs had just lined up a shot he had no hopes of making. Before he attempted it, he paused to chalk his cue by grinding it into the plaster of the ceiling like the barbaric cit that he was.

Gerry gritted his teeth into a smile and retracted his sympathy for the man. Then, without a word he offered Carstairs the cube of white chalk that sat on the table's edge. He would have to come back in daylight to assess the damage to the ceiling. Judging by the current company, there were likely years' worth of marks left by men that had no sense of how to deport themselves outside of a public billiard hall.

For now, he would enjoy the surprised look on Carstairs's face as his ball rolled just short of its mark and stopped.

Ronald's response was to pot two balls in one stroke and finish the match.

'Game to me,' he said with a smile.

'You are a damned lucky fellow,' Carstairs said, wiping his brow and reaching for a pad and pencil to write a marker of his debt.

'Very lucky,' Ronald said, feigning modesty.

'But I will allow that I have some skill in the game.'

'You must play me next,' Gerry said, finishing his drink in one gulp and giving the broad smile that he knew made him look like a simpleton. 'I have not played in ages. There was no time for games in Wellington's army.'

'Well, then. This should be interesting for both of us.' Ronald's smile was positively wolfish as he chalked his cue.

Gerry turned to the rack and chose a mace instead. The old club-headed sticks were horribly out of fashion. But he was as good with one as he was with a cue and they overcame the deficiencies of the table quite nicely.

Ronald arched an eyebrow in surprise and replaced his cue, as well. 'My, but it has been a while since you played.'

'When Father taught me, it was with wooden balls so lopsided there was no telling where they would go, even at the best times.' As if demonstrating, he swung the mace wide, nearly knocking a drink from the hand of Wilson, who was standing too close to him.

'You'll find that the new ivory balls work much

better,' Ronald said, setting up his first shot and tapping the red ball with his white one.

'I expect so,' Gerry said and deliberately missed, sending his cue ball bouncing off the padded rail. Then he looked up and smiled. 'But we have not set a wager yet.' He brought the mace up so quickly it set the oil lamps above the table to swaying.

Ronald sent Gerry's cue ball rolling into a pocket. 'Nor have we set the points. Play to six?'

An easy thing for him to say, when he was already up by four. Gerry smiled broadly again. 'Excellent. And let us make it interesting. Fifty quid?'

'Fif...' The wind was escaping from Ronald like gas from a balloon. 'I do not have so much ready money.'

'Fifty from me, then,' Gerry said. 'And if I win, you may forgive the debts of the men who have played so far. That should call it even.'

'If you really think that is wise,' Ronald said, pityingly.

Gerry grinned and nodded like a fool. Then, with a single stroke, he sunk all three balls with a cannon, to the calls of 'Capital shot' and 'Huzzah for the captain!'

'And how many is that, again? I cannot remember.' Gerry counted points on his fingers.

'Ten,' said Ronald, his smile disappearing. 'Game to you, sir.'

'It is all a matter of geometry, dear fellow. Back in the day, I was quite good at mathematics. The markers, if you please.' Gerry held out his hand for the IOUs and his brother-in-law handed them over with a frown.

Gerry tore them in half with a single decisive motion and dropped the pieces on to the table beside him. Then he yawned. 'And now, I think it is time that I retire.'

'You must not,' Carstairs said. 'The night is just beginning.' By the slur in his voice, the night had gone on far too long already.

'I have been away from home and wife for seven years,' Gerry said. 'She will not want me lingering with the gentlemen until dawn.'

'A lovely woman she is,' Burke announced. 'And a shame that she has been alone so long.'

Gerry felt the hair at the back of his neck prickling as if it could rise like the ruff of an angry dog. How many other men had noticed Lillian's beauty and made drunken comments over the billiard table about her sleeping alone? And what sort of man was Ronald North for showing not a hint of disapproval?

'Those days are now past,' Gerry said and gave Burke a look that brought a mumbled assurance that no disrespect was intended.

He nodded and looked past the man at Ronald. 'I am home for good.' Then he stared into his brother-in-law's eyes to be sure the idiot noticed that there was a wolf beneath the sheepskin. 'I will be with her, until death us do part. Just as I am sure you intended when you introduced us.' Then he quit the room, ignoring the low curse behind him.

Chapter Seven

Once upstairs, Lily put on her best nightgown and allowed the maid to put a ribbon in her braided hair. By the smile on Jenny's face, she could guess that the girl was imagining the fond reunion to come.

The ribbon was superfluous. She doubted it would matter to Captain Wiscombe how she looked. Despite what her father and brother believed, Gerald's reasons for lying with her had nothing to do with romance. He was merely staking a claim of ownership.

Would that her own motivations were as clear. She could tell herself that going to his bed tonight was nothing more than an attempt to be the loyal wife he'd deserved from the first. It would have been much easier to believe, if both her father and brother had not reminded her that she was a North and therefore an expert manipulator. Was she being her usual, obedient self and doing what Gerald wanted her to do? Or was she following her family's instructions and doing what might make him do what she wished at some later date?

Or was this about nothing more than her fascination with Captain Gerald Wiscombe, late of the Fifth Dragoons? Her only experience with what went on in the bedroom had left her with no desire to repeat the act. But after years of reading about his exploits, the thought of Captain Gerald Wiscombe made her heart flutter in anticipation.

There was fluttering in other places, as well. Her husband was not some paper idol. He was here and all too real. And tonight, she would finally be his bride. Suddenly, it felt like her chaste cotton night rail was made of butterfly wings. Each shift of cloth on skin reminded her of just how bare she would be when he removed it.

For a moment, memories from the past clawed at her mind like a rat in a cage. The headache, which had eased during the quiet hours since dinner, began to return.

She took a slow breath to clear her head. The past was the past. Tonight would be different. There would be no fear or guilt since the man involved was her husband. Not only that, the man she had married was a romantic daydream come to life. There was not a braver or more honourable man in all of England than Gerald Wiscombe and there were few men as handsome.

If only he didn't hate her...

After what seemed like hours of silence, she heard the hall door of the room beside hers open and close. There was no second voice, or any other indication that he'd summoned a servant to help him prepare for bed. In fact, there was no sound at all. Had he forgotten about her already and gone to sleep?

It would be better to face her fears and seek him out than to lie awake in her bed, waiting for a summons that might never come. It took a few more minutes to steel her nerve before she tiptoed across the floor of her room to the connecting door and opened it, just a crack.

'Come.' It was a command. The first of many, she suspected. As a good wife ought, she obeyed it.

Perhaps the wine at dinner had mellowed him. Except for his boots, he was still dressed and stretched full length upon his bed, staring at the canopy above him. Compared to the scowls of the afternoon and the guarded smiles of dinner, he looked at peace with himself and the world.

It would be a shame to ruin that for either of them. She had the sudden, craven desire to retreat.

'I thought you had a headache,' he said without looking in her direction.

'It is better,' she lied. Now that she was in his room, it was coming back again.

'Then do not hang about the doorway. If you are coming in, come in.' He did not finish with the suggestion that she should do it or go away, but it was implied.

So forward she went, into the room, shutting the door behind her. *A different man*, she reminded herself. *A different room.* Or it might as well have been. She had made sure that nothing remained of the old master bedroom but her memories.

He turned away from her to stare at one of the pictures on the wall, giving it far more attention than a simple landscape deserved. Were the details in some way wrong? Most likely they were and he was making a note to have the thing removed and replaced.

The one thing he did not seem interested in was her. She had not expected him to spring upon her like a wild beast and force her on to her back. But neither had she expected uninterest. She felt like a fool standing here in her simple gown and her sad little hair ribbon. He did not want her. Now that they were alone, there was no reason for him to pretend otherwise.

He sighed as if her presence in the room was an interruption and looked back to her, then gestured absently to the side of his bed closest to her own door. When she did not move, he prompted, 'Get in.' Then he sat up and untied his neckcloth without bothering to see if she complied.

Before he could ask again, she pulled back the coverlet and climbed between the sheets, resisting the urge to pull them up so she might hide under the blankets. It was not as if there was anything to see, should he decide to look. Her gown was buttoned to the throat. But it proved one thing to both of them. She was not planning to bend him to her will through seduction. If she'd intended that, she would have done a better job of preparing for it.

Her husband sat on the edge of the bed, his back still to her. When he pulled his shirt over his head, she got her first look at a man's naked back. She could not help it. She gasped.

'Eh?' He turned with a half enquiring, half annoyed look.

'The scar.' She pointed.

His face softened, then he laughed. 'It is not a very heroic story, I'm afraid. A screaming Frenchman was galloping down upon me from behind. On seeing that my attention was elsewhere, my friend, MacKenzie of the Scots Greys, shot him in the back. It was too late to stop the full charge. He did not run me through as he'd planned. But the damned frog dragged the blade down my back as he fell and cut my coat to ribbons. It was some time before we were able to dress the wound, which was hardly deep enough to care about. I stripped off what was left of my shirt, and Mac poured a measure of his usquebaugh on my back and a wee dram into me. Then I sewed up my jacket and slept on my stomach for a week.'

'That is all?' she said, surprised.

He nodded. 'If it bothers you, then I suspect you will be even more disturbed when you see the rest of me.'

She had been thinking just such a thing when trying to imagine him naked.

He laughed again and gave a lascivious waggle of his eyebrows to show that he had been talking of other scars, but knew full well what she'd been thinking.

She shrank a little farther under the covers. The papers had said nothing of such things. They'd left her to imagine entire scenarios based on the phrase *heroic charge*. 'Were you injured often?'

He gave a non-committal shrug as he pulled off his stockings and threw them towards the wardrobe. 'As much as anyone, I'm sure. But not as much as those who did not come home.' Then he stood, turned to face her and displayed his chest. There was another cut across his upper arm, but it was clear from the wide scar that this had been deeper than the one across his back.

And lower, just above his waist, was a puckered puncture.

He pointed. 'This is the one that should have done for me. A hole in the guts is a damned ugly way to die. But it managed to miss my vitals and come right out the other side. Of course, you won't see that until I take off my breeches.'

'But you recovered,' she said with a sigh of relief.

'I was feverish, of course. But I fought it off and was back in the saddle in a month and a half. The surgeon said it was a miracle. I assume I should be thanking you for your prayers for my safety.' He said the last with an ironic twist of his lips.

For all she knew, it was exactly how he had survived. Would he believe her, should she tell him so? 'I prayed fervently for your good health each night for seven years.' When she saw the answering glare, she added a smile as ironic as his had been. It seemed to satisfy him more than her sincerity.

'And now you have got your wish.' He undid the buttons on his breeches, dropped them to the floor and kicked them out of the way as he pulled back the bedcovers and climbed in beside her.

She had known for some time that it would not be the soft dumpling of a boy who came to her, should her wedding night ever occur. But she had not been prepared for Gerald Wiscombe in the flesh. Even flaccid he was a formidable specimen. His lack of embarrassment at his own nakedness made him all the more intimidating.

Despite the scars, he was also blessedly intact. She'd seen more than her share of veterans of the Peninsula walking the halls of the Chase on wooden legs and crutches, or with empty coat sleeves pinned up to keep them out of the way. But whether from luck or answered prayers, her captain had returned with two strong arms and two good legs.

Now that she could see all of him, she'd noted the tracery of smaller scars that accompanied the major wounds. This was a man who viewed injury as mere inconvenience, should it stand in the way of what he wished to achieve. Once he had begun, resisting would be futile.

For a moment, the old fears returned and she

shrank back even farther towards the edge of the bed, glancing towards the door of her room.

He made no effort to reach for her. 'You may leave if you wish. I have no intention of holding a wife by force, especially you.' Then he rolled on to his stomach. 'Or you might make yourself useful and rub the knots out of my shoulders. After three days in the saddle I am as stiff as an unsoaped harness.'

'H-how would I do that?' It was an unexpected request. But it would be less frightening to do than to be done to.

'It will not be difficult. Begin by putting your hands about my throat and pretending that you wish to choke the life out of me.' He laughed into the pillow.

She could not see his face. But by the tone of his voice he seemed to be honestly amused by the idea that she might want to hurt him. At least he trusted her enough to turn his back to her while naked and defenceless. She responded to his trust with her own and pulled her legs up under her to kneel at his side. Then she placed her hands on his shoulders and began to knead.

It was easy to see why he'd wanted her help.

The muscles beneath her fingers were as hard and unyielding as bags of sand. Or perhaps that was normal. She had never touched so much bare male skin in her life. As she worked over them, she felt the flesh begin to soften and relax.

Her own tension was easing, as well. The warmth of his body and the rhythmic kneading of her own hands worked as a soporific. The last of the pain in her head diminished to a dull throb, then disappeared.

It was replaced by hesitant pleasure. She liked touching him. There was something very comforting about the feel of his warm flesh beneath her hands, as if he could transfer his bravery to her through the skin. She wanted to curl up next to him, to press her cheek into his shoulder and stay there until the world felt right again.

In response to her massage, her husband grunted in satisfaction. 'You are almost as good at this as an army leech. Of course, he used horse liniment.'

In spite of herself, she smiled. Then she dug her fingers more deeply into the space beneath his shoulder blades. 'I am sure we can find something better than camphor and turpentine to use in the bedroom. My maid has a recipe for a balm made with beeswax and peppermint…'

He was laughing again, his shoulders shaking with mirth. Then he gave a lurch and rolled, catching her wrists and pulling her off balance and on to her back. 'By all means, we must render me sweet-smelling if we are to share a bed.'

The sudden change in position left her breathless and light-headed. But this time it was a good feeling, more like floating than fainting. There was something about his smile, so close above her, that kept her from being afraid. She answered him with a hesitant nod.

He leaned on his elbows so that he might look down into her eyes. 'You are a comely wench, Lily Wiscombe.' He ran a fingertip along the line of her jaw. Then his smile was coming closer and his lips met hers.

Wiscombe.

She was not a North any more. She was a Wiscombe. One of two. Soon, two would become one. If it was anything like this kiss, she had nothing to fear. His mouth was open and his lips moved slowly against hers. Very gently, she reached out with the tip of her tongue to taste the crooked smile and the tiny imperfections that made him so fascinating to look at.

In response, his body stirred. His arms tightened around her. Their breath mingled in a sigh.

'He mounted his horse in the night at the door,
'And sat with his face to the crupper.'

The song, bawdy and off-key, came like a nightmare interrupting a dream. Mr Carstairs was in his cups, and walking down the corridor of the family wing at the worst possible time.

Her mind immediately flew to the hall door of her own room. She replayed the memory of locking it after her maid left. She'd set the key upon the dresser, just as she did every night. She was safe.

But that room had never been the problem. This was the room that was dangerous. It might look different, but underneath the paint and paper it was the same. And the doors here were not locked as they ought to be. Anyone might enter from the hall. Her head was pounding now as she waited for the sound of a hand testing the handle.

Her husband pulled away from her, staring at the door. 'What the devil…?'

'Some scoundrel has cut off the head of my horse,
'While I was engaged with the bottle…'

The song was even louder now, even closer. But she was not alone this time. And it was not just her husband come too late to save her from dishonour. Her hero, Captain Wiscombe, was finally here and bristling with righteous anger.

Suddenly, her fear of the drunk in the hallway seemed overblown. She touched her husband's bare arm. 'It is nothing,' she said, praying that was true. 'If we ignore him, he will go away.' She would lie awake the rest of the night fearing that he, or someone else, would return. But as long as Captain Wiscombe was here, she would be safe.

'Which went gluggity, gluggity, glug.'

All the same, she could not seem to control her body's response. She was trembling, quite out of character with the foolishness of the song.

Please let him go, she entreated silently. *Please.* The day had been hard enough without this.

'Enough.' Wiscombe pushed away from her and swung his legs out of the bed, reaching for his breeches.

'It is nothing,' she repeated, if only to convince herself.

'It damn well is not. It is Carstairs. The man is a bloody nuisance,' he said, throwing a shirt over his head and pulling boots over his bare feet. 'Despite what may have been condoned in my absence, my home is not a tavern and my bedroom is not a music hall. I mean to put a stop to it.' Then he was through the door and it slammed behind him.

"'Tis strange headless horses should trot,
'But to drink with their tails is a—'

The song came to an abrupt end and the silence was profound. She waited, breath held, to see what would happen next.

The minutes had stretched out into an hour and still nothing happened. The singing did not continue, but neither did Captain Wiscombe return. Had he locked the door when he'd gone? She stared across the room, at the door handle, watching for movement.

She debated the sense of slinking back to her own room so that she might safely lock herself inside. Then it occurred to her that, should someone look for her, this was the one place they would not search. Even if they suspected that she was here, they would not dare enter the bedroom of a decorated soldier. She was safer in Wiscombe's room than she had been in her own.

The thought was strangely comforting. She was in her husband's bed, where she belonged. She eased back into the pillows and pulled the coverlet up. Then she closed her eyes to rest them until her husband returned.

Chapter Eight

When Lily woke the next morning, it was in her own bed. She lay perfectly still for a moment, trying to dredge up the memory of the previous evening. Had she roused sufficiently to get herself here, or had she fled? If so, had it been before or after her husband's return?

She searched both her body and her mind for any trace of disturbance that could explain this situation. She was a sound sleeper, particularly after a megrim when she had been stressed to the point of exhaustion. But if Captain Wiscombe had returned to bed her, she'd hoped she would have some memory of it.

It appeared that he had returned to find her sleeping and carried her to her own bed without waking her. She had a vague recollection of arms lifting her up and a sigh of soft breath at her temple. It seemed he had chosen to prolong this part of his homecoming for another night, at least.

She rang for her maid. As usual, she selected a day gown that was both simple and sensible. Her father sometimes accused her of dressing no better than an innkeeper's wife. When he did, she invariably told him that since he insisted on housing strangers in her home, she saw no reason to behave as if she were entertaining friends.

But this morning, when she went down to breakfast, she would be greeted not just by her father's friends, but by the critical eye of her husband. She rejected the first gown and chose a snow-white muslin with a wide border of violets embroidered about the hem. There were purple ribbons at her waist and she requested that Jenny thread more of them through her curls. When they were finished, she looked as fresh as a spring morning.

Before he'd arrived, she'd imagined what it might be like if the past between them did not exist. Suppose they had never married and she was meeting Captain Gerald Wiscombe for the first time at a ball or garden party. This was the way she would want to look if she wished to capture the attention of the hero of Salamanca.

Against all reason, her stomach filled with hopeful butterflies. Things had seemed different last night. Though he had refused to discuss the war while at table, he'd been willing to tell her about his injuries. While she had been touching him, he'd been happy and content, as had she. Perhaps this kernel of trust might grow to be something more.

Would he notice a difference in her look or manner when she arrived at the breakfast table? If he did, he did not say. There was no indication that he approved, other than a slight raise of his eyebrow as he examined her over his coffee cup. When he smiled, it was the same false grin he had been using at supper. Whatever truce they'd achieved while together in the bedroom did not extend to the other rooms of the house. 'Good morning, my dear.' His voice was just as dispassionate as his expression.

She could answer in kind. But if she wished for a change, there was no point playing games with him. She gave him her warmest smile and curtsied. 'Good morning, Captain Wiscombe.'

'I trust you slept well?'

Was he asking because he had put her to bed, or was it nothing more than polite conversation? 'Yes, thank you.'

'I suspect it was difficult because of the noise in the hall.' This was said to no one in particular, as if he meant to call the perpetrator to task over it.

'That was Carstairs,' her father announced, as though there were nothing particularly strange about drunken serenades. 'We really must teach the man a new song.'

'Or teach him to sing the current one correctly,' Ronald added. 'He cannot seem to hit the high note, for all the times he tries. I see he is sleeping late this morning.'

'Perhaps feeling the ill effects of the bottle,' Mr Burke added.

'He is not sleeping late,' Mrs Carstairs announced. 'At least he is not doing so in our room. He was not there at all last night.'

All assembled shifted in their chairs, trying to

pretend that they were not hearing accusations of infidelity over breakfast.

The offended wife's gaze swept down the table, searching for signs of guilt. 'Miss Fellowes is not present, either.'

Mrs Burke made sympathetic noises of disapproval.

'Neither is Sir Chauncey,' her father supplied. 'Perhaps Miss Fellowes is with him.'

'What would they be doing together so early in the morning?' Mrs Wilson's smile was positively evil.

'I am sure they are both in their own rooms where they belong,' Lily said, trying to stop the rampant speculation. 'And Mr Carstairs...' Really. She had no idea. 'Perhaps Mr Carstairs is hunting.'

'If he is, he must be told to leave the old stag for me,' Greywall announced to no one in particular. 'That fellow is mine.'

'I do not think that is the game he is after,' said Mrs Burke with a sniff. 'More likely he has caught a young doe.'

Mrs Carstairs hissed through her teeth and

pushed away from the table as if preparing a physical response to the insult.

Before Lily was forced to intervene, there was a shriek from the hall and the sound of breaking glass. The residents of the breakfast room hurried to the doorway, eager to see what fresh scandal was brewing.

All except Captain Wiscombe. He merely helped himself to more fish and refilled his coffee. She left him to it and followed the others into the hall.

Once there she found something far more interesting than the gossip over last night's serenade. Mr Carstairs was standing in the hall, sporting a blackened eye and naked as a jay except for the silk runner he had seized from a nearby side table. Sally, one of the younger and more impressionable parlourmaids, was collapsed in a dead faint, surrounded by the sherry glasses she had been retrieving from the parlour.

'I had no intention…' stuttered Mr Carstairs. 'I awoke in a horse trough in the stables. But my clothes…I do not know… And there was a black stallion snapping at my…' He gripped the table runner even tighter over his unmentionables.

'Was the trough not full, then?' Wiscombe said innocently. He stood at the back of the group, coffee cup still in hand. 'Poor Satan must be starving. I will go and speak to his groom.' He passed his drink to an approaching footman and walked past the shivering Carstairs as though he did not see him, muttering to himself about the need to set in a decent supply of oats and mash.

Since Mr Carstairs had been just outside their door before the singing stopped, Lily suspected that her husband knew perfectly well about the condition of the horse trough, the source of Carstairs's black eye and the location of the gentleman's clothes. But if he did not wish to speak of them, neither did she.

She pushed through the knot of guests blocking her way and went directly to the maid, who needed more help than her embarrassed guest. She positioned herself so that Sally would be spared from witnessing more nakedness if she woke. Then she called for a footman to bring a glass of water and spirits of ammonia.

Behind her, in the doorway to the breakfast room, Mrs Burke could no longer contain herself. Her stern disapproval of moments earlier dissolved and she let loose with a braying guffaw worthy of Satan the stallion. Mr Burke joined her, as did the earl. Mrs Carstairs answered them with a torrent of words that no lady should know.

Phineas North made a desperate attempt to re-establish a semblance of decorum and tried to shoo the ladies back towards the table. But no amount of gesticulating and tut-tutting sympathy from her father could quell the general mirth at the poor man's misfortune. With a moan, Mr Carstairs fled for the stairs, the table runner fluttering behind him.

Mr and Mrs Carstairs left later that day, citing urgent business in London. Gerry smiled to himself as he watched from his bedroom window and saw the carriage disappearing around the last bend of the drive. He had been successful in removing the first two interlopers. The rest would follow soon enough.

A single punch to the eye had been enough to stop the singing. But Gerry had not wanted the man sleeping off the liquor on the floor of the hall, only to awake unabashed and resume the song. He'd deemed it best to provide a lesson that could not be unlearned. He had thought about the matter for less than a minute before his own infernal sense of humour had taken hold. It had ended with him carrying the man like a sack of grain out to the stables, stripping him of his garments and leaving him.

He had not intended to abandon his wife. It had just taken more time than he'd planned to settle with the drunk in the hall. He'd meant to return to Lily with an amusing story to tell. When he'd left, she'd been shaking beneath the covers like a half-drowned puppy. He'd felt almost sorry for her.

Before the interruption, things had been going better than he'd expected. He'd had a damned fine reason for his foul temper yesterday afternoon. But the satisfaction of besting North at billiards had improved his mood. Retiring to that most suitable of bedchambers to have his shoulders caressed by a ministering angel had left him as tame as a kitten. To finish the night with his needs satisfied and his head pillowed on a soft breast would have made a fine end to a difficult day.

Then Carstairs had come and ruined everything. He'd lost his temper and the lady had lost her nerve.

By the time he'd got back to his room Lily had been fast asleep, curled into a ball beneath the blankets as if she feared attack. It had been an impulse to carry her to her room and put her to bed properly. There, she had settled in her own place with a happy sigh and continued sleeping.

What was he to make of her strange behaviour? When he'd imagined his return to Wiscombe Chase, he had assumed his wife was as conniving and crooked as the rest of her family. She would come up with a dozen unlikely stories for the condition of his house and the child presented as his heir. Perhaps she would try to seduce him into forgiving her. He would allow her to attempt it, at least for a time. She might be faithless, but she was every bit as beautiful as she had been on the day he'd married her. Back then, he'd been too embarrassed by his own inexperience to take what was his by right. Despite himself, he still wanted her. He would not miss the opportunity again.

But she was not the scheming jade he'd expected. Her dress was modest, her manner apologetic and obedient. At dinner she'd remained polite but aloof from the dinner guests. He wondered if she had feigned illness to escape them. When she'd come to his room, there had been no sign of the chronic headache that had been described to him by her brother.

Instead, she had been concerned and sympathetic to his injuries, old and new. She had talked of beeswax and peppermint, hinting at massages to come. And she had returned the kiss he'd given her.

She had been cautious of him, but not frightened. She had not shown fear until they'd been interrupted by the man wandering outside in the hall. But why? Carstairs had been no threat at all. He was just a jolly drunkard who could be tricked by his own weakness. It served him right for treating his hostess's hospitality with the same contempt he had for the billiard-room ceiling.

This morning, it pleased him that Lily had needed no instruction to hold her tongue. She'd taken her cue from his indifference and pretended there was no logical explanation for the naked man in her hall. But he suspected she had been amused by it. Had he seen a faint flicker of a smile on her lips as she'd rushed to help the maid?

She approved. Her approval should have meant nothing to him after all this time. But it did.

But he had far more approval in this house than he really wanted. He frowned down at the paper on the writing desk that sat under the bedroom windows. When he'd returned to his room after breakfast, he'd found it on the rug in front of the door, as if it had been slipped beneath to lie in his path as he entered.

The rectangle of parchment was folded once, the crease bisecting the writing with a razor-sharp line. Opening it revealed the multiplication table copied out in ink. It would have been an exaggeration to call the writing neat. There were smudges and blots, and a few grains of sand still clinging to the drying ink. But it was hard for a small hand to manage a pen. At that age he'd been using pencil, or chalk and slate.

This was clearly an attempt to impress him. And damn it all, he did not want to be impressed. He wanted to forget the one doing the writing so he might enjoy his new life at home. He wanted to clear the house of undesirables and stare into Lily's soulful brown eyes and pretend that she had never betrayed him. That would be impossible with a child underfoot, trying to get his attention.

He crumpled the paper and turned to throw it in the grate. Then, something stopped him. Too much work had gone into the preparation of this gift. While he did not want it, he would feel guilty if he destroyed it. Perhaps the child's mother would wish to see proof of the boy's educational success. He smoothed it flat again and tucked it between the pages of the *Théorie Analytique* where it would be out of sight until he was ready to deal with it.

He smiled down at the books. They were just the sort of gift he appreciated. How had she known he would want them? For that matter, how had she known to do any of this? Did she have some ingrained talent for homemaking and hospitality, to turn his detested childhood home into such a welcoming place?

Now that he'd got a look at it in daylight, he was even more eager than he had been to evict the guests, so he might enjoy his home in peace.

The old heap of stone was comfortably familiar, yet so very different from the way he remembered it. It had been a sad house when he'd left it. Generations of neglect had worn on it, making it seem not just old, but tired of spirit. Even on the best days, there had been an odour of rank greenery and loam about the place, as if in a few more years the forest would reclaim the land and leave nothing for the last of the Wiscombes.

Now, even standing by the open windows, the air seemed fresh and cool. Lily and her horrid family deserved some credit for chasing out the dampness, fixing the roof and giving it all a wash and a coat of paint.

Then he reminded himself that if the other Norths were involved, the spaces outside his bedroom had not been done for his benefit. There was a plot in progress and he was tired of feeling as if he'd wandered in on the last act of the play. It was time for Lillian to prove her loyalty and tell him what had been going on here.

To find his answers, he left his room and took the stairs down to the wing that was the ladies' side of the house. There was no such thing, really. But his family had traditionally split itself along the line created by the centre hall. The billiard room, the library and the trophy room were to the left. The breakfast room, the morning room and the conservatory were to the right. Generations of Wiscombes had found that, if one wished to, one could avoid one's wife most of the day, except for dinner and the bedroom. A man's life could be largely unchanged by marriage if he had the sense to stay on his own side of the hall.

In his youth, Gerry's father had limited himself to half the house, even after his wife had passed. While Gerry kept the memory of his mother alive by haunting the spaces that had been hers, Father had treated the right side of the house and the son in it as if they no longer existed.

If the current lady of the house truly wished to avoid her houseguests, she must have fallen in with Wiscombe tradition and retreated to the wing not littered with empty wine bottles and dead deer. As Gerry turned down the right hallway a young face peeked out from behind the curtains in the hall, then disappeared again.

It was the boy. It explained the feeling he'd

had all morning that he was being watched. The sounds of scrabbling and rustling that he'd heard while touring the ground floor earlier had not been mice in the wainscoting. It had been but a single pest, following behind, waiting for an invitation to come closer and discuss the gift.

When he was young, Gerry had tried such tricks on his own father and had been consistently rebuffed. The elder Wiscombe had had little use for anyone not old enough to take up a weapon and follow him into the field for a hunt. But at least Gerry had been the actual heir. It was annoying that this little whelp who had no claim of blood thought he was entitled to attention.

He did his best to ignore it. But now that he had recognised it, the sound of shifting feet on the hall rug behind him was maddening. At last, to no one in particular, he said, 'Go away.'

There was a sniffle in response.

Children's tears were even more annoying than women's. Especially when they were someone else's children and none of his concern. But it was not the child's fault that he was a bastard. It would be unfair to treat him too harshly. 'And well done on the mathematics,' he added, without turning around.

The sniffling stopped. There was a sigh, then the shuffling receded down the hallway.

Very good. He had no time to deal with a single mouse when the whole house was full of rats. He continued down the hall. Gerry checked the morning room, and music room, and salon, but found them vacant. This left him with the biggest folly of his foolish house: the conservatory.

Father had claimed that no true Wiscombe cared a fig about plants, on a plate or in a pot. So it had been the first space to fail after his mother had died. With its cracked panes and overgrown tangles of ivy and ferns it had sat for years like a cancer in healthy flesh, letting the noxious wildness into the rest of the house, as if the woods themselves had come to take revenge for the continual disturbance of the wildlife.

But when he entered today, he was struck by the fresh smell of lemons on the two dwarf trees that flanked the entrance and the sweet spice of geraniums and gillyflowers in pots by the windows. Sunlight streamed through the glass roof and walls, which were both clean and unbroken.

The beams shining though the green glass panes that decorated the walls cast a mottled pattern on the veined marble floor that resembled a carpet of fallen leaves.

In the midst of it was the fairest flower in the house: his Lily. She had not yet noticed him enter, so he used the opportunity to observe her. Did she know that the midday sun behind her shone through the muslin gown to reveal far more of her figure than he had seen last night while they were in bed? A thin layer of gauze and a few embroidered flowers were all that stood between him and the paradise of her high, full breasts, round hips and shapely legs.

Seven years' bitter experience separated him and the naive child he'd been when he'd married her. Yet, when he looked at her he felt the same tightening in throat and groin that he'd experienced on the day he'd met her. He'd known that they were not making a love match, despite what her father claimed. What would a beauty like her want with a nothing like him? But perhaps, if he returned to her with a chest full of medals and a full purse, she would look at him with something other than frustration and disappointment. What a fool he had been.

As if she had heard his thoughts, she looked up at him now and gave a little gasp of shock. She dropped the bamboo-handled paintbrush she had been holding and it rolled across the floor to stop at his boot toe.

He stared down at it in surprise. Just now, he'd been too preoccupied by her figure to notice the easel she worked at and the watercolours on the glass-topped table beside her. It should not have surprised him. All ladies had hobbies and this one was not uncommon. But it had never occurred to him that *his* wife would have interests, other than spending his money and making him miserable with her infidelity.

Without a word, he picked up the brush and went forward into the room to give it back to her.

'Thank you, Captain Wiscombe.' She gave a nervous curtsy and cast her eyes downward, as though not quite sure how to respond to his sudden appearance.

His mind was equally unsettled by her demure response. 'You paint?' It was good that he had not been trying to impress her. He'd never have done it with such a fatuous remark.

She shrugged, embarrassed. 'Watercolours, mostly.' When pressed to make conversation, she seemed just as awkward as he felt.

He glanced down at a tall stack of books and newspapers beside the paints. A closer look revealed them to be a mix of atlases, gazetteers and histories of Spain, France and Portugal, along with several old copies of *The Times*. 'And these?'

'Inspiration,' she said and almost knocked over her water glass as she tried to hide the clipping on the top of the stack.

He was faster, holding her wrist with one hand and snatching up the paper with the other. He scanned the text, reading a few lines aloud. '"And notable for their valour in the charge was the troop led by Captain Gerald Wiscombe..."' He put the paper back on the table and smiled at her. 'You find me inspiring?'

She shrugged again, blushing. 'I followed the news of the war. It would have been foolish not to. And while flowers are lovely, one can only draw so many of them before it becomes tiring.'

A feeble excuse from someone who was obviously enamoured of the dashing hero the newspapers had made him out to be. He'd met such women before. He could set them to giggling and blushing with a single smile. An invitation to hear a few of his tamer war stories would end with them sitting indecently close, his arm draped about soft shoulders in reassurance as sweet lips offered rewards for his bravery.

He looked at the woman before him, *his woman*, and stifled recollections of his romantic past with an embarrassed cough. He released her hand. 'And what is your current project?' He glanced at the work in progress. 'Mont-Saint-Jean?' He could not keep the surprise from his voice.

'It is only a copy.' She pointed to the open book beside her paints.

Perhaps it was. But the style of rendering was familiar. 'You did the paintings in my room?'

'It seemed like a sensible place to put them,' she said. 'At least until something better could be found to decorate the walls. I hesitated to choose permanent ornaments without your input. I will remove them, if you like.'

'No,' he said hurriedly. 'Your work is surprisingly accurate for someone who has never visited those places.' He glanced back at the picture in the book. 'See here?' He pointed. 'You've changed the angle of the light and captured the colour of it in a way this pencil sketch did not. And in the pictures in my room you've found the wild beauty of the countryside and omitted the chaos and blood that we left. It is how I want to remember the places I've been. The pictures are perfect just where they are.'

'Perfect,' she repeated, surprised.

'I like them well, as I do the rest of the decoration. Is that also your doing?'

She gave another shrug. 'I merely chose the things I imagined a man such as Captain Wiscombe might appreciate, after reading accounts of your bravery.' Her gaze dropped even farther, as if she were fascinated with the toes of her own slippers. 'You were quite famous, you know.'

'I did nothing that other soldiers wouldn't have done in my place.' If she would giggle or flirt, he might be able to respond in kind. But the earnestness of her praise embarrassed him. While in the thick of the action, he'd never intended to be a hero.

'On the contrary, the papers said Captain Wiscombe showed singular bravery, charging ahead when others retreated.' Now that she'd admitted to her preoccupation with his career, she gathered the nerve to look up at him with wide-eyed awe.

'You talk of this Wiscombe fellow as if he is some sort of paragon that a lady might swoon over and not standing here in front of you.' He looked at her, waiting for her to laugh at the hyperbole.

Instead, the blush in her cheeks turned scarlet. She could not seem to utter a syllable in response. This was no common infatuation that might be appeased with a single kiss on the cheek. She might have stood yesterday's criticism with cool grace. But today, she was suffering an agony of mortification over gentle mockery.

Had she really created an ideal of him in her mind and doted on it, just as he'd hoped she would? If so, it was too late. Her loyalty was worth nothing if she'd only found it after she'd betrayed him. But staring at the half-finished picture on the easel, he felt the anger beginning to drain out of him, just as it did when he entered his room the previous evening. He looked away.

'Whatever the reason for your painting,' he said gruffly, 'you've done well by it. And the bedroom you've prepared for me is quite the nicest I have been in. It suits me. Do not change a thing about it and hang as many pictures there as you care to paint.'

'Very well, Captain.' With her assent, she seemed to stifle her more tender feelings with the unquestioning obedience he'd requested yesterday.

She must not give up so easily. 'We will admire them together tonight,' he reminded her, flashing his most devilish grin. It was unfair to toy with her, but he could not resist.

'Yes, Captain.' This time, the breathlessness in her voice stole his own, as did the thought of this beautiful creature in his bed. It would be just as he dreamed of, after all. Once he'd chased the last of the guests from the house, they would be able to explore their passions in private.

And then he reminded himself that she and

her family had been instrumental in gathering the people he must now evict. While they might have stopped the leaks in the roof, they'd let Greywall into the house, allowing the one thing he'd hoped to avoid by accepting wife and commission.

While his wife's devotion to him was flattering, it was a new thing compared to the loyalty she'd shown to her conniving father and brother. Though Lily was beautiful, sometimes poison could be hidden in a pretty bottle. He should have better sense than to drink it.

'I did not come here to speak of my war record, or your feelings about it,' he said, crushing the fragile rapport between them. 'I want you to tell me what is really going on in this house.'

'What, exactly, do you wish to know about?' He watched the blush fade from her cheeks, revealing the cool, distant woman who presided over his dinner table. Her question was not an evasion so much as a request for clarification.

He gave it to her. 'What are your father and brother doing in my house, and who are these guests they have invited here? And what does it have to do with their initial eagerness that I marry you?'

To his surprise, she looked almost relieved that he had asked. 'My father makes regular trips to London, where he has ingratiated himself into the sorts of circles where there is too much ready money and very little standing in society. When he has found three or four fellows who seem interested in changing one for the other, he invites them to a house party.'

'You cannot buy rank,' Gerry said with a shake of his head.

'You did,' she pointed out. 'Father often opines that it would be better if society worked as the military did. There would be room enough at the pinnacle if it were easier for men of vision to pay their way up to being gentlemen.'

'Perhaps so,' he acknowledged. 'But that is not the way of things.'

'But suppose there was an opportunity to dine in intimacy with a member of the peerage. A friendship there might result in other invitations and a chance to move in more august circles once one returned to London.'

'Greywall,' Gerry said with a frown.

'An earl could be kept like the bear in the Tower of London,' she agreed.

'As if my neighbour was ever of real benefit to anyone,' Gerry said sceptically. 'And what does your father gain by this far-fetched altruism?' It was a question he should have asked himself when offered a beautiful wife and a commission. 'Does he charge admission?'

'That would be too obvious.' She waved the hand that held the brush as if painting the truth in the air. 'The gentlemen who visit are better at making money than friends.'

'They are drunken louts,' Gerry agreed.

'It makes them susceptible to offers that appear friendly, especially when they include a chance to make even more money. After a few days spent bagging partridges and chasing foxes, and a few nights drinking good wine, they are offered an opportunity that cannot fail to profit. My father thinks of them as investors.'

'Investors,' Gerry repeated. 'In what?'

'I believe the current offering is the breeding of Russian sables,' Lily responded with a sigh.

'That is the most ridiculous thing I have ever heard.'

'So you would think. But it has worked several times before. The first time, he bought an actual pair of the animals to bolster the plan.'

'The first time?' he said, amazed.

'It seems the sable farm is doomed to failure. The first pair escaped into the woods and have been—' she gave an embarrassed cough '—fornicating with martins and not each other.'

'If he has no sables, how can he convince anyone of the viability of this plan?'

She gave a small shrug. 'Does a Londoner know what a sable looks like before it has been made into a coat collar? A stoat dyed black will do just as well.' Now she was smiling. 'Ronald got a rather nasty bite during that process. Apparently, stoats do not enjoy being dipped.'

'Is that your brother's sole part in the scheme, the painting of weasels?'

She shook her head. 'My father is a man of big ideas. My brother less so. He enjoys cards and billiards. Any game of chance, really. He invariably wins. That is why Greywall is here. At this point, I believe we own more of his estate than he does himself.'

We. Had she even noticed she'd said it? Possibly not. But it annoyed him that as she'd explained her family's plans, she'd grown more animated and the colour had returned to her cheeks. 'That explains your father and brother,' he said. 'The guests and the earl, as well. But what is your part in all this?'

Her smile disappeared. 'Recently? I am hostess. Nothing more than that. I make sure the house is maintained. I avoid the guests as much as I am able. I do not approve of what is happening here. Really, I do not.' The protest was adamant, but it came far too late in the conversation.

'But that is, as you say, recently. What was your part before?'

'To be pretty and biddable,' she said, her eyes falling. 'To marry where I was told and not ask questions.'

'You were bait for me,' he clarified.

'To make the plan work, they needed the earl. He is your neighbour.'

'And he has coveted this house since my father was alive,' Gerry added.

'He wants the stag that has been roaming your land for ages.'

Gerry nodded. 'My father called him Rex.

King of the forest. I saw him in the woods as I arrived.'

'Wanting a thing is different from getting it,' she replied.

'I am aware of that.' He looked at her and thought of his own marriage and what that first decision had gained and lost him over the years.

'They wanted you so they might get the house. They needed the house to trap the earl. The earl attends these parties to reclaim his markers from my brother.'

'And his presence attracts your father's investors from London,' he finished.

'As will yours, if they are allowed to continue,' she whispered, glancing at the door as if she feared to be overheard. 'My brother thinks he will convince you that you owe them for the improvements made on the house. If that does not work, he will find some other way to trick you out of your money. Father assumes I will help them because I am a North. And the Norths always look after their own.'

She looked so dejected at the thought that his common sense fled, just as it had on the day he'd met her. 'Then it is a good thing you are not a

North,' he reminded her, taking the paintbrush from her hand. 'You are a Wiscombe now.' Then he tipped her chin up so that he might kiss her.

In Portugal, he'd often regretted that he had not come to her on their very first night as man and wife. He should have claimed her as his own immediately. But kissing her today, the remorse faded. Without having known others, how would he have recognised the sweetness of her kisses? Her mouth opened to him with the slightest coaxing. As he drank deeply from it, her body settled against his, ready to submit.

His hands were resting on the bare flesh at the base of her neck and he felt the pulse beating against the tips of his thumbs grow faster. He squeezed her shoulders in encouragement before smoothing his palms over and down her back, pressing her breasts and belly hard against his chest. At last, he reached the flare of her hips and her rounded bottom. He first cupped and then kneaded the flesh until she was squirming against his budding erection, gasping in eagerness.

He would have her here, naked as Eve in the Garden of Eden. He could imagine trapping her against the windows, his palms pressed flat to the cool glass. The scent of lemons would mingle with her musk as he thrust. And her cries...

Her cries would alert the household. He did not give a damn for any of the people here. But it would be more enjoyable to act out this particular fantasy once he had divested the Chase of the excess inhabitants.

He tightened his hands to fists, digging his nails into his palms to distract him from the temptation of her body. Then he moved his hands back to her shoulders and gently pushed her away. It pleased him to see that she looked as disappointed as he felt by the end of their play. But it was not nearly as nice as it would be when they had time to continue.

He cleared his throat and smiled. 'As I said before, tonight we will have time to discuss the pictures that are hanging in my room.'

'Yes, Captain Wiscombe,' she said with a dazed smile.

'And we will discuss your concerns about the future, as well. But do not worry, Mrs Wiscombe.' He added a slight emphasis to the surname, so she might remember it. 'Since there are but two of us Wiscombes, we must stick to-gether.'

'Three.' The child's voice came from the door-way, breaking his mood like a stone through window glass. 'There are three Wiscombes, Papa. Do not forget me.'

He had, damn it all. Just for a moment, he had forgotten the boy. But his memory had re-turned and ruined everything. He shot a word-less glare at the woman before him. Then he turned, pushed past the child and was gone.

Chapter Nine

No matter what he intended, Gerry was far too quick to play the fool for this family. A few daubs of paint, a doe-eyed glance and a pair of soft lips and he had been ready to forget the obvious, until it had intruded on him and demanded his attention.

He must not be swayed by appearances. The woman he'd married was as crafty as Eve, just like the rest of her family. But if she was to be any use to him outside the bedroom, it would be easy enough to prove. He crossed the length of the house to his study, pulled the chequebook from the desk drawer and wrote a hurried draft. Then he went in search of his brother-in-law.

'Ronald North.' He found him in the billiard

room and greeted him with the same joviality he had on the previous night.

'Wiscombe.' The memory of the previous night's game must have been fresh in his mind, for he did not bother to be pleasant.

'Practising for a rematch?' Gerry said, picking up a ball from the table to spoil the shot. 'I would think, after years of chasing Rex about the wood, you would know that it is very hard to beat a native habitué of the Chase at any game played here.'

'It was never my intention to best you,' Ronald said, with a smile. 'There is no reason we need to be at odds. We are family now, after all.'

'By marriage,' Gerry reminded him. 'And while I am grateful for the help you provided with the house and lands, I suspect you must be growing tired of the place and eager to get back to wherever it was you came from.' He pulled the cheque from his pocket and held it out to his wife's brother. 'This should cover the cost of repairs made to the house and the commission your father bought. I have added an expression of my gratitude for your help, as well.'

The look of shock on Ronald's face was most

satisfying. It was clear that he would not have thought to ask for this much, had he carried through with his original plan. Now, he was torn between pocketing the money and looking for the catch hidden within the offer.

'There should be enough here to find a place of your own, if you do not already have one,' Gerry added. 'Dear Lily and I are eager to begin a private honeymoon, now that I am returned.'

Ronald withdrew his hand. 'You and Lily and Stewart, you mean.'

And there was the boy again, in the way even when he was not here. 'We are speaking of you at the moment,' Gerry reminded him, dragging the conversation back to where it belonged. 'I suspect it will be very dull for you, once your friends are gone. Unless you wish to spend your future evenings playing Spillikins with us.'

Ronald laughed. 'No guests and nursery games? Are you going to tell me you had no time for cards in the army?'

'I am as skilled at them as I am at billiards,' he admitted. 'But I do not like them overmuch, since the time I was forced to challenge an acquaintance for cheating at the table.'

'A rather extreme reaction for what was probably a mistake on your part,' Ronald said, watching him closely.

'On the contrary, it was the other fellow's mistake.' He smiled, baring his teeth. 'He didn't have an opportunity to make another.'

'And what does this story have to do with anything?' Ronald asked, impatient.

'It is merely to inform you of the future of Wiscombe Chase,' Gerry said. 'No guests. No cards. No hunting either, for that matter. Nothing but peace and quiet from here onwards.' He held out the cheque again.

Ronald took it from him, ripped it in half and handed it back to him. 'Do not insult me, sir.'

Gerry grinned back at him. 'If you find this insulting, you have much to learn, Ronald. Let me know when you have found a place to settle. We will need the direction so we can forward the mail.'

'I do not think Papa likes me very much.'

After the captain had left them, Lily had struggled to calm her racing heart. It was not just the touch of her husband's hands that left her feeling naked and exposed. She thought he'd uncovered everything about her, from the reason for their marriage to her devoted reading of his war exploits. Then Stewart had come into the room and reminded them both that there were some secrets still remaining.

Even though the captain was no longer in sight, her son was staring back down the hall, hoping he'd return. It had been foolish of her to feed the child on tales of the hero of Salamanca. Had she honestly thought that an outpouring of devotion from the boy would result in answering love from the man?

Of course she had. It was different for women. She had not wanted a child, either. At one time, she'd even planned to send him away, never to be spoken of again. But once he'd arrived she could not manage to do it. He was harmless and blameless and he needed her. More importantly, he was blood of her blood, closer to her than her father and brother would ever be. Stewart was the only person in the house, perhaps the only one in the world, who truly loved her without boundary or question.

Now she came forward to take him by the

hand, leading him away from the doorway to their favourite place, a bench by the window that was all but hidden by large ferns.

'Papa does not like you?' She put her hand in the middle of his back and felt the trembling that was a first indicator of tears. It would be even worse for them both if the captain realised that he had been burdened with what some might call an overly sensitive child. She rubbed his shoulders, soothing him until the tremor passed and he was calm again. 'I think it is too soon to make such judgements against him,' she lied. 'He has been home but a day. You barely know each other.'

'Before, in the hall, he told me to go away,' Stewart said.

'And so you followed him into the conservatory?' Lily could not help but smile.

'I did not know he would be here,' Stewart argued.

'But he thought you disobeyed him,' Lily said gently. 'That might be the reason he seemed angry.' One of the reasons, at least.

'He was kissing you.' Now militant anger was banishing the doubt.

Here was another thing she had not thought to prepare him for. 'Yes. And he will do so again. At least, I hope he will. I quite like it when the captain kisses me.' Finally, there was a bit of honesty in the conversation.

'Do you like it better than when I kiss you?' Worry was creeping back into the boy's voice.

'It is a very different thing when you kiss me. I like your kisses, as well.' She turned to him, held out her arms and was rewarded with a wet kiss on the cheek. She kissed him back on the top of the head and smiled down at him so he might see nothing had changed between them.

Stewart frowned back, unimpressed. 'Well, I do not like it when he kisses you. If anyone must go away, it should be him. At least he could stay away from the conservatory. That is our place. He can have the stables. He likes horses. I do not.'

This was another problem that she had not dared mention to the cavalryman. The only time they had tried to put him in the saddle, they'd found Stewart a mare so placid it should have been no more dangerous than riding the parlour sofa. And yet she had dumped him into the first hedge and broken his collarbone. Stewart did not like horses and, as far as anyone could tell, the feeling was mutual.

'It does not matter if you like horses or not,' she said, hoping it was true. 'I suspect he would rather you not ride at all than that you do so simply to hunt foxes. He seemed most disapproving of that activity at dinner last night.'

The boy brightened a little.

'And we cannot send Captain Wiscombe away,' she added. 'This is his house and he is quite eager to stay in it, after so long away.' But her husband was far less eager to share the house with the child at her side. How could she ever explain it to Stewart in a way that did not break his heart?

She gave him an encouraging smile. 'But for now, you must do your best to be patient with the captain. I am afraid he does not know very much about the likes and dislikes of little boys.'

Stewart frowned. 'He should know more than you. He used to be one.'

That was true enough. But it did not sound as though his childhood had been a happy one. 'When he was young, things were very different. The captain's father was very strict and sent him off to school at a very young age. He was not allowed home, even for holidays.'

'But he would not do that to me, would he?' he asked in a frightened whisper. By the look on Stewart's face, he could not imagine a worse fate than the one that might very well be his immediate future.

'Of course not.' Perhaps she was not a North. No member of family had ever been as unconvincing a liar as she was now.

Despite her efforts to hide it, Stewart had glimpsed the truth. 'But if he wanted to, you would not let him,' he said and stared up at her, desperate for reassurance.

If her husband insisted, what choice would she have but to obey? How would she survive when he was gone? What meaning would life have if she regained the love and trust of her husband by sacrificing the child who had loved her without question from his first breath?

'Of course not.' She kissed him on the top of the head so that he could not see the fear in her eyes. 'Do not worry about the captain, or anything else. I will take care of him and you.' She would find a way to make this work. She had to. 'But for now, do not cling to his heels. Give him time to recover from his travels. I am sure everything will work out for the best.'

She must have grown more convincing with practice. Her son nodded to her and gave her a small smile and another hug.

She smoothed his hair. 'Now back to the nursery with you. It is almost time for lessons and you do not want to keep Miss Fisher waiting.'

When he had gone, her brother stepped forward from the other side of the fern. 'Everything will work out for the best?' He applauded her with a series of slow claps and an ironic smile. 'A touching performance, Lillian.'

'It was not a performance,' she whispered, glancing towards the hall to make sure her son had not heard.

He laughed. 'It was made up of whole cloth to keep your son from crying.'

She walked across the room to shut the doors so there would be no further interruptions. 'He is just a little boy. What would you have me do?'

'You could tell him that his position here is even more precarious than yours.'

'What good would that do, other than to frighten him?'

'At least it would be honest. You should have told him the truth from the first. You should not have raised him to idolise a man who is not his father.'

'When did you become a champion for the truth?' she snapped.

'When did you become so good at lying to yourself?' he countered. 'You are pretending that it will be possible to resolve the problem of Stewart with time and patience.'

'Stewart is not the problem,' she said, closing her eyes so she would not have to see the smile on Ronald's face.

'Of course not,' he said, suddenly gentle. 'Gerry Wiscombe is. If he'd had the decency to die as expected, we would not be in this mess.'

'You mustn't say such a thing.' She opened her eyes again to stare past him, at the door.

'Do not lie and say you never thought it yourself.' Ronald moved in front of her so she could not avoid his gaze. 'Admit it. Life would be easier for Stewart if your husband was dead.'

It would. But she would die herself before she

said so. 'I will not choose between my husband and son. And if you and Father have plans for Captain Wiscombe, you should not be wishing him dead.'

'We had plans,' Ronald said, almost too sweetly. 'But just now, he caught me in the hall, grinned like an idiot and, without so much as blinking, offered me ten thousand pounds for the repairs done on the house. Then he asked me where our future home might be, now that we would no longer be able to entertain here.'

'Did you take the money?' she said, hoping that, just once, her brother would do the sensible thing and admit defeat.

'Of course not. We can make ten times that if we stay here. But how did he know to bribe me? Did you tell him of my plans?'

She said nothing, for it was clear he knew the answer.

Her brother nodded, as if he had expected her silence. 'It is clear that we cannot trust you to be loyal to your family, even though it is in your best interest. So, dear sister, I will make it easier for you.' There was something dangerous in his offer of help, like the warning hiss of a snake before the strike.

'What do you mean to do?'

He smiled again, and waved a warning finger. 'If I tell you, Lillian, you will pass the information on to Gerry, just as you did before. You've done enough tattling, so I must give you a reason to stop. If you offer him so much as a word of warning that something is afoot, I will track down young Stewart and tell him everything that you have not.'

'You would not dare.' But, of course he would. After a lifetime watching her brother take advantage of others, there was not a doubt in her mind that he would hurt a child to further his ends.

'If you wish to test me, talk to your husband. Ask the heroic Captain Wiscombe to protect the boy from me and see what that gains you. He cannot stand the sight of the child. He might even applaud my effort to clarify Stewart's position here.'

'He would never be so cruel,' she said.

'Put him ahead of your family again and we

shall see. Or do what you should have done from the first. Hold your tongue and trust that we will take care of you, just as we always have.'

Chapter Ten

With the absence of the Carstairs, the upstarts at his luncheon table had each moved a seat closer to the head of the table. Against all decorum, Miss Fellowes still held the spot on his left, while Mrs Wilson had taken the right. While the married lady seemed more interested in the wild boar and mushroom pie on her plate, Gerry was beginning to worry that Miss Fellowes intended to make a meal of him. He'd noticed several accidental touches of his sleeve at the beginning of the meal. Now that they were finishing, he felt the gentle pressure of a knee against his own.

He shifted to the right to evade her and stared down the dining table at his wife. If possible, she was even lovelier than she'd been in the conservatory. There was still a pleasant flush in her cheeks from the kisses he had given her. And though her throat was bare of ornament, he could not seem to tear his eyes away from it. He wanted to touch his tongue to the faint pulse beating there, to make it race as he seduced her. If he was not careful, he would give himself over to her, body and soul, as he'd been ready to do this morning.

At least, until her son had interrupted them and brought him crashing back to earth. How had he managed to forget about the one obstacle in their marriage that was all but insurmountable? Even if he managed to rid the house of the child, there was the question of inheritance. He must see if it were possible, at this late date, to deny parentage of the boy, if only to protect any real offspring they might have. The longer he waited, the worse it was likely to be for all concerned.

Laws being what they were, it might be easier to disown a legitimate child than cast off his wife. Now that he was here, and could look into her huge brown eyes...

It was lust. That or stupidity. When he held her, he forgot to be sensible. Her obvious attraction to him made it even more difficult to control himself. And her willingness to share her family's secrets left him with the illogical hope that there might be no more lies between them.

The stunned look on Ronald's face when he'd offered to buy him off had done much to justify the hardship he'd endured to get the money. Ronald would live to regret that he'd refused that offer. The alternative methods of ridding himself of the Norths were far less pleasant than bribery. And with Lillian's continued help he would be one jump ahead of her brother at every turn.

'Will you be joining us in the sitting room this afternoon, Captain Wiscombe?' Miss Fellowes batted her eyes and closed the distance between them again. 'The gentlemen have declared the day too wet for a hunt. And last night we ladies missed your company.'

From the end of the table, Sir Chauncey noticed the attention Gerry was receiving from his light o' love and shot him an icy glare.

Apparently, the insolent puppy did not realise the insult he had given, bringing a whore to a house party. Gerry ignored him and awarded her his most empty-headed smile. 'Of course,

Miss Fellowes. My wife will be joining us, as well. She is fully recovered from last night's headache.'

Lily's mouth had already been open to refuse, but she read the look in his eyes and closed it slowly, forcing a smile. 'Of course, Captain. I am looking forward to it.'

'I imagine you are,' he replied. But something was wrong. The skin about her lips was white with tension and her brow was furrowed. Perhaps her megrims were genuine. If so, she must learn to ignore them. Tonight, he would speak to her about the need to be socially available, in case he needed her help. If she did not like the people her father entertained, she must see that avoiding them and hiding in her room had done nothing to reduce their numbers. The way to conquer adversity, or a gaggle of unwanted house guests, was to meet it head on.

After the last of them had finished their meal, they adjoined to the sitting room and the ladies requested a table be set up so they might play loo.

'Captain Wiscombe,' Mrs Burke called, 'you

must open your purse wider for your poor wife. She refuses to bet with more than sixpence. If there is so little in the pot, it is hardly worth playing.'

There were mutters of agreement from the other ladies, and another longing look in his direction from Miss Fellowes. Lily frowned at her cards, but said nothing.

Gerry ignored her and the Fellowes woman, and gave Mrs Burke a sympathetic smile. 'I am afraid there is nothing to be done about that, madam. Lillian is far too sensible to listen to me on a subject as important as money. I cannot seem to hang on to that from one day to the next.'

'Then you must come talk to Mr North,' Mr Wilson called from the middle of the discussion on the other side of the room. 'He is the sort of brilliant businessman who can turn one pound into ten in the blink of an eye.'

'Or ten pounds into one,' Greywall added. Ronald North leaned across the card table and filled his glass before he could speak again.

'I will be careful not to close my eyes if he is near my purse,' Gerry said.

The elder North gave a merry laugh as though the comment did not bother him in the least. 'You have nothing to fear from me, Captain. I would not encourage others to invest in some of my riskier endeavours. It would pain me greatly if anyone incurred a loss while following my advice.'

'What sort of investment might that be?' Apparently, Mr Burke was the sort of man who could not tell the difference between a warning and a welcome. Nor could he recognise the obvious trap being set for him.

'My current venture is far too likely to end in failure,' Mr North demurred. 'Of course, the odds might improve if I was able to raise enough capital to do the job correctly...'

'Tell us more,' Wilson encouraged.

'Yes, Phineas. Tell us more.' By the sound of it, the earl had said his line so many times that he'd lost the ability to sound sincere. Ronald refilled his glass again to keep him quiet as North continued his pitch.

'As you can see from the magnificent pelts that are displayed in the trophy room, the land surrounding this house is teeming with wildlife.

Beaver, badger and otter all but walk into the traps set for them. But suppose it were possible to catch fur-bearing animals and breed them? We might be hip-deep in skins before the winter season. Tailors and hat makers in the city would take as many as we could supply.'

'You mean to breed beavers?' Miss Fellowes was staring at him with wide eyes.

Mr North shook his head. 'They are fine animals, of course. But if one could find a flock of Russian sables...'

'Are they measured by the flock?' Gerry interrupted.

'I have no idea,' North said, then continued. 'If I could acquire a pair of sables, house them, feed them and encourage them to mate...'

Miss Fellowes giggled.

'But where would you get Russian sables?' Gerry asked.

'From Russia,' Ronald snapped, staring at him as if trying to gauge whether he was the stupidest man in the room, or the most devious.

'I have already imported the first pair,' Mr North admitted.

'Let us see these wondrous animals, immediately,' Gerry said with a smile that should have put Ronald on guard.

'I do not know if that is wise,' his father-in-law said with a worried smile. 'They are very delicate creatures. Any disturbance can interfere with their breeding.'

'But it is daytime.' Gerry reminded him. 'Surely they breed at night like good Christians.'

Miss Fellowes giggled again.

'Perhaps. But in daylight, they are rather excitable,' North said. 'And prone to biting.'

On the other side of the room, Ronald flinched. Lily held her cards up to her mouth, probably to disguise her smile.

'Perhaps it will help if I speak to them in Russian,' Gerry said. 'I know a few words. I will tell them that we mean no harm.'

'But we do mean harm, if we wish to make coats out of them.' Mr Wilson glanced out at the rain and looked longingly back at the card table.

'Then I will be forced to lie,' Gerry said cheerfully. 'Let us go out to the stables at once. If they are going to make us all rich, I must see these little foreigners immediately.'

At the mention of riches, Wilson changed his

mind and called for hat and umbrella. Even Sir Chauncey set aside his jealousy and agreed that a little fresh air would be an excellent idea.

They set off a short time later, stumbling through the mud towards the cluster of wire-mesh cages standing at the back of the stables. 'Are these they?' Gerry asked, pointing to the two forlorn animals housed there.

North beamed. 'The pride of the Urals. My supplier assures me that they can have up to a dozen kittens a year. It would be better if there were more pairs, of course. It strengthens the bloodline.'

Without waiting for further explanation, Gerry unlatched the door and thrust his gloved hands in, dodging needle-sharp teeth to grab the animals by their necks. Then he pulled them from the cages and held them out, one in each hand, so all could see. 'Say hello to the fellows, Mr Sable. We are all eager to meet you. And Madam Sable, as well.'

Then he gave a dramatic pause. 'What ho, Madam? What have we here?' He held the animals out to Wilson. 'Do you see what I think I see, sir? Surely I am not mistaken.'

Wilson leaned forward and then back again as the animal hissed. 'I do not think it likes to be examined, Captain.'

'None of us does,' Gerry replied with a smile.

'Let me see.' Miss Fellowes stepped forward.

'This is not...' Gerry stopped himself. He had been ready to say that it was not a sight for a lady. But since the caution did not apply to Miss Fellowes, it hardly mattered.

The woman in question saw what he had and turned away with a giggle.

'What the devil are we looking at?' Ronald said, angry that he did not see the source of the mirth.

Gerry turned to North, the stoats wriggling in his hands. 'You are right, sir, when you say the investment is a risky one. The person who sold these animals to you has sent you two stallions and no mares.'

'Males?' The shock on Ronald's face at this revelation was quickly turning to anger.

North had an entirely different reaction. 'Two males.' He laughed. 'Well spotted, Captain.

There is no cheating a man with such sharp eyes.' He laughed again and patted his belly, as if he'd just eaten a full meal and been well satisfied. 'Would that I'd had your perspicacity. It seems I have been duped by a wily trader.'

And there was the secret of North's success. Even caught in the act, he was so good-humoured about it that one wanted to believe he was not at fault. 'I recommend that you write to Russia immediately and take the supplier to task over this,' Gerry said, feigning earnestness.

'I will indeed,' North agreed.

'Males,' Ronald repeated.

Lily, who had skirted the edge of the crowd as they'd approached the cage, was nowhere to be seen. But Gerry thought, from somewhere on the other side of the stables, he heard a peal of feminine laughter.

On the way back to the house, North hung back from the rest of the party and Gerry lagged, as well. They waited until the rest were well out of earshot before either of them spoke.

'Ronald underestimates you,' North said, the half-smile never leaving his face.

'At his peril,' Gerry agreed. 'To save us both further embarrassment, I will not denounce you publically. But I trust I will hear no more about turning my home into a sable farm.'

'There is always the ruby mine in Brazil,' he said wistfully.

'Brazil is known for emeralds, not rubies,' Gerry pointed out.

'All the more reason to invest in the rubies,' North replied. 'When we find them, they will be twice the value of emeralds.'

'And if you do not find them?'

'Mining for gems is a dangerous and difficult thing, under the best circumstances.'

'But even if the investors are left empty-handed, I suspect you will still come away with a tidy profit.'

'There is no reason for me to bear the whole cost of a failure,' North said. 'The whole point of having investors is to minimise liability, should something go wrong.'

'I would hope that it is a way to share profits, as well,' Gerry said. 'Should I examine the schemes you have backed since taking residence here, I would bet not a one of them succeeded.

But despite all these failures, you are able to fill the wine cellars and entertain.'

'Perhaps I am merely unlucky,' North admitted. 'But I have managed to make the best of my failures.'

'Perhaps you auction seats at my dinner table as though you were trading horseflesh at Tattersalls,' Gerry announced. 'And while you peddle weasels dipped in boot black, your son sharps at billiards and cheats at cards.'

'The people who come here deserve what they get,' North said. 'They are trying to find a route to wealth and status that does not involve hard work. We both know that is not the way the world turns.'

'Did I deserve what was coming to me when you tried to swindle me out of my house?'

North paused to look him up and down. 'When I found you, you were an impoverished student with a ruin of a manor. Now you are a rich man and respected by all in Britain for your heroism. The house is still yours, as is my only daughter.'

'I could just as easily have died penniless,' Gerry said.

'But you did not,' North reminded him, smiling.

Gerry stared back in amazement. The man was truly a master manipulator. North was looking at him with the grin of a proud father, doting on a son's success.

Gerry offered no smile of gratitude in return. 'You are trying to persuade me that the last seven years has been a boon and not a hardship. Do I need to remove my shirt and show you the battle scars?'

'If you do, I will show you a mirror, so that you might see the positive changes the army has wrought in you.'

Arguing with the man was like trying to hold an eel. 'I admit I have changed. But it was not necessary for me to join the army to do so. There is no telling what might have been, if you'd just let me alone.'

North snorted. 'I will tell you exactly what you'd have done. You'd have ended up a Cambridge mathematics tutor married to some parson's pinch-faced daughter.'

'I would never...' But it was an accurate assessment of the future he'd planned for himself, before Phineas North had stepped in and upended his life.

'Eventually, you'd have been forced to sell this house to Greywall. I know for a fact that he wanted it. And I know you refused.'

'Because he hounded my father into the grave trying to get it,' Gerry admitted. 'I did not particularly like my father. But I like the earl even less.'

'He is a rather unlikeable fellow,' North admitted.

'But I did not need to go to war to keep the house out of his hands. If all you wished was the use of it, I could have just as easily rented it to you. Or sold it to you, for that matter.'

'I could never have afforded to bid against an earl for the purchase of this place. It was cheaper to buy a commission than a house,' North said, beaming. 'So I gave you an opportunity. You used it as an honourable man would and made a success of yourself.'

'But you could not have known the outcome,' Gerry insisted.

'I beg to differ,' North said. 'To do what I do, one must be a good judge of character. While I am sorry to admit that both of my children doubted your chances of survival, I knew from the first that you would return to us. Today, you proved that you are the sort of fellow who sees stoats when others see sables.'

'I had Lily's help with that,' Gerry admitted.

'My darling girl.' North's smile broadened. 'Such a daughter is a father's proudest achievement. A jewel as pure as diamond and more valuable to me than all the emeralds in Brazil. I am glad to have found a man worthy of her. Even without her warning, you'd have seen my sables for what they were. You, Captain Wiscombe, are a man of vision. You see a move ahead of the other fellow and behave accordingly.'

Then why did he have such difficulty reading his own wife? 'If that were true, I would not have listened to you in the first place.'

'On the contrary. Even as you agreed to my offer, you knew it was too good to be true. I read it in your eyes. But you wanted Lily and you wanted a chance to prove your worth to yourself, and to her. So you weighed the risks and said yes.'

It was true. He had known that something was not right about the marriage. But the benefits of the commission had outweighed any potential problems.

'You must admit, now that it is over, it has turned out splendidly. You are home safe to your beautiful wife and adoring son. What more could you want?'

He did not know.

When Lily had insisted that no one knew the true origins of Stewart, he had assumed that she was lying. But by the look on North's face, he honestly believed Stewart to be legitimate and that his daughter was a faithful wife. It would be a bitter enlightenment when the truth came out, but it could wait until after he and his son had been extracted from the house.

Gerry cleared his throat and forced himself to answer. 'What more could I want? There is one more thing I want and I will have it with or without your agreement. I want a quiet and empty house. I will have no more parties like this one in my future. There will be no more breeding of sables and no mining for rubies, emeralds or any other non-existent stones. If you attempt this scheme or any other, I will stop you. And the next time I will not bother to be subtle about it.'

'Very well.' North sighed.

'You may tell your son that I will permit him to play billiards, as long as the table is properly maintained. But if I discover he is cheating at cards, he will think fondly of the days when the worst he'd experienced was a bite from an angry stoat.'

North nodded in approval. 'It is a shame we cannot convince you to join in the fun. As a mathematician you could have a natural talent for calculating odds and angles.'

'I am not sure that is the compliment that you mean it to be,' Gerry said.

'Take it for what it is worth,' North said, with a wave of his hand. 'But know that, if we were to do it all over again, I would gladly give my daughter's hand to such a man as you.'

'To get my house,' Gerry finished for him.

North shook his head and gave Gerry a sad smile. 'Because her heart was never in these little games of mine. Her disapproval has only hardened with the passing of time. She will hardly speak to me any more. Since you would rather risk your life in service of the crown than cheat your fellow man, she will be much happier with you than with me.'

The affirmation had touched Gerry's heart and his mind was crowding with ordinary responses about being a worthy husband for the man's precious daughter.

Then he remembered that none of the Norths were to be trusted. Phineas's fine words about his daughter did not explain a bastard son and years gone by without so much as a note. 'Do not worry about Lily. For now, think of your own future, and accept that, wherever it might lead you, it will not be Wiscombe Chase.'

Chapter Eleven

By the time they arrived back at the house, Gerry was feeling well and truly pleased with himself. North was not such a bad fellow, once he'd been persuaded to move on. The guests seemed to have lost interest in cards and were either seeking naps in their rooms or by the fire in the sitting room. While Ronald North was still somewhere causing trouble, things were not the muddle they had been just two days before.

But it seemed he had lost his wife again. Lily had left the house with them when they'd set off to visit the sables. But she had disappeared before the matter was settled. It seemed she was available only when necessary, there one minute, gone the next. Would she be more accessible after the others were gone, or would it be like living with a spirit who had to be conjured and bound each time he wanted her?

Perhaps she had gone back to the conservatory. The afternoon light was not nearly as good as that in the morning. But when he turned towards the ladies' wing, he came face to face with her noxious little boy who was, as usual, roaming the house and ready to spoil his mood.

Stewart stood frozen in the middle of the hallway like a marble statue.

Gerry stared, waiting for him to move.

He made no effort to do so. 'Mama said I was not to follow you about.'

Gerry continued to stare. 'You mother is an intelligent woman. You should listen to her.'

'I am not following you,' Stewart said. 'I am in front of you.'

The boy had a point. While he'd met officers that thought they could lead from the rear, it was much harder to follow from the front. 'Do you have lessons to do?'

'Already done,' the boy said, giving no quarter.

'Perhaps you need a nap,' Gerry suggested.

The boy shook his head. 'Adults take naps. Because they are old. Do you need a nap?'

'Perhaps I do.' But it had not been his intention to take it alone.

'You should do that, then,' the boy said and turned to walk into the conservatory.

Gerry sighed. If Lily was in the conservatory, there was little hope of privacy, short of grabbing the little beast by the collar and hauling him back to the nursery. Such an act would not endear him to the boy's mother. In truth, he would have little respect for himself after. He had learned from his own father how it felt to be punished for the sin of existing. He would not inflict that on another.

All the more reason that Stewart should be sent away to school. Since he was young, he would adjust quickly to his new surroundings. He would find friends, teachers and the company of good books. When he was old enough to understand, Gerry could explain that it was nothing personal. He would be provided with an education, an allowance and a trade. But there could be no future for him here.

Today, he could have the conservatory, if he wanted it, and the company of his mother.

He sighed and made his way to his side of the

house and the trophy room, thinking it might be nice to pass some time in the small library beyond it. If there was any room that the current guests had no interest in, it was probably the one that held books. In truth, the library had got little use when the Wiscombes had been the sole occupants of the house. His father had made sure that the room that displayed the majority of the heads and horns held pride of place before the rest of the rooms on the main floor.

What his father had viewed as a convenience, Gerry considered an obstacle to progress. It seemed impossible to get so much as a cup of tea on the gentlemen's side of the house without walking by the trophy room door or passing through it to get to the opposite hall.

But today, there was reason to pause. Apparently, he had been wrong about the location of his wife. The sound of a woman singing drifted through the open doorway. He stopped to listen.

'I would love you all the day.
'Ev'ry night would kiss and play,
'If with me you'd fondly stray,
'Over the hills and far away.'

The tune was the same as the song they sang in that old comedy about the recruiting officer, telling men to leave their brats and wives and take the king's shilling. But these words were a hundred times sweeter and he let himself be wooed by them.

From now forward, if he ever had to wander the hills, they would be close to home, not far away. He'd stay with the woman who loved him. He stepped through the door to declare himself. 'I'm here, darling. And come to collect, if that song is an offer.'

'Captain Wiscombe?' The singing stopped. Miss Fellowes appeared from behind the torso of a steinbock that Father had dragged back from an excursion to the Alps.

His smile froze in place. 'Miss Fellowes. My apologies. I thought...' Stuff what he thought. With the look she was giving him he was for-given for the mistake. He strode towards the door on the opposite wall that led to the library.

'Don't go.' She hurried across the room to stand between him and his goal. 'I have hardly got the chance to talk to you, even though you are my host.'

'I have been home but a day,' he reminded her. 'I've barely spoken to my own wife yet, much less talked to...' He'd been about to say 'unwelcome guests' and barely caught himself in time. 'I was just looking for Lillian.' He turned to retreat the way he'd come so he might continue to do so.

She countered to stand before him again, blocking the way to the door. 'I was so excited when I heard we would be coming to your home. But I had no idea that we would actually meet the great man himself.'

'It was a surprise to me, as well,' he said, looking longingly past her at escape.

'And for a chance to hear the tales of your exploits...' She clasped her hands in rapture.

'They are hardly stories that I would tell a lady,' he said, although there was much doubt as to how much of a lady this woman was.

'I am sure the accounts in the newspapers do not do them justice.' She pressed her clasped hands under her chest and sighed. The amount of bosom this displayed at the neckline of her gown was too impressive to be anything but a calculated move.

But for a moment the cheap trick worked. He was distracted.

'You deserve to be rewarded for your bravery,' she said, stepping closer.

'No reward is necessary,' he replied automatically, dragging his eyes back from her breasts to her face and taking a step back into the room.

'The gratitude of a grateful nation is hardly enough.' She beamed at him, more pleased than offended by his attention and took a step to close the distance between them.

'It is more than enough for me.'

'The Regent made Wellington a peer,' she argued.

'I am no Wellington.' He took another step away.

'Only one of his most courageous horsemen,' she said, coming even closer.

'I don't need…' He was backing hurriedly towards the library door now and glanced behind him to be sure of the direction.

'But, I insist.' In that moment of inattention, she pounced.

He was growing soft from inactivity. On the battlefield, his reflexes had been faster and he'd have been smart enough to keep his eye on the enemy. He certainly hadn't displayed any of the foresight that Phineas North had credited him with.

But a single kiss from a pretty woman was hardly a matter of life and death. She was a comely thing and her eagerness hinted at rewards far beyond a quick tussle in a common room. Perhaps, if circumstances had been different...

There was a crash from the doorway to the hall.

He broke from the Fellowes woman and looked up to discover the cause. His own wife stood frozen in the doorway. A broken vase was at her feet and a bouquet of camellias was scattered beside it.

The Fellowes jade looked up as well and gave her a flushed and triumphant smile.

In response, Lily made a sound that was almost a whimper and muttered her pardon. Then she bent to scoop up the flowers and stuffed them, stems and blossoms awry, back into the vase. Water ran through the cracks in it, staining her gown. She dumped the mess on to the hall table only to see it totter on its broken base and almost fall twice more before she could steady it enough to let go and escape down the hall towards the stairs.

The lock to Lily's room turned with a satisfying click, sealing her away from the mortification awaiting her in the rest of the house. For a moment, she leaned her forehead against the silk-covered door panel, as if it were as possible to draw strength and comfort from the wood beneath.

How could she have been so stupid?

She had known in her heart that her husband had not been faithful to her while he was gone. After seven years apart, there was no chance that he'd return as the same awkward innocent. He had been tricked into the marriage and there had been no guarantee that he'd live to return. She could hardly fault him for a lack of fidelity.

But she'd chosen to imagine that once he'd returned home, if he forgave her at all, he'd want only her. He had thought her beautiful, once. For him, she'd worked hard to maintain an illusion of youth that was becoming increasingly hard

to cling to. She did not deserve to see him turning to younger, prettier women within a day of
his arrival.

When had she become so foolish? He had told
her on the very first day that this was not to be
the case. But then, he had said, *if I tire of you.*
Could it really have happened so soon? It did
not matter. There was no sense in being hurt. He
would do as he pleased and she had no say in it.

Before they'd married, she'd been sensible.
She'd understood that her life was out of her control. But while he'd been gone, she'd convinced
herself that if she was pretty and biddable, eventually she would get what she wanted, as a matter of course. He would come back, sweeping
into her life like a rescuing knight. He would
forgive her trespasses, banish her troubles and
they would live together, happily ever after in
the home she'd prepared for him.

Perhaps she had been imagining Lochinvar.
Captain Gerald Wiscombe was no romantic hero
who would give her her dreams. He was a man.
Therefore he was just as uncaring, cruel and
faithless as all the others.

The worst of it was, she had embarrassed

herself by showing that she cared. When she'd caught him in a tryst she should have had the sense to withdraw quietly. Instead, she'd called attention, fumbling with that vase and drawing out the retreat. Now she was hiding in her room in a sodden gown, too humiliated to have a maid see her crying.

It was nearly as bad as the worst night of her life. Then, she'd lain shivering in her bed, unwilling to call for help. She had told no one. When she'd realised that she was with child, it was easier to stay silent than to admit that she had been so foolish as to leave her door unlocked in a houseful of drunken men.

But brooding on the past did not change the fact that she was cold and wet right now, and had likely ruined her favourite day gown. Tugging at the bodice would rip the muslin and make matters even worse. She straightened, stepped away from the door and stretched her arms to the middle of her back. Then she clawed helplessly at the tiny mother-of-pearl buttons, only to stomp her foot in frustration when she could not manage them. And now the tears were falling faster.

'Let me help.'

Captain Wiscombe had followed her to her room and she had been so upset she had not even heard him enter through the connecting door. 'I do not need help,' she lied, refusing to turn and face him so that he might see her tears. 'Not from you. Not from anyone.'

'I disagree.' His voice was surprisingly gentle, as were the hands on her back, undoing the buttons of her gown. Once it was open he lifted it over her head and she watched out of the corner of her eye as he walked across the room to drape it over the door of the wardrobe. Then he returned and undid her petticoat so she could step out of it.

Now she was standing in nothing but stays and shift, and shivering from reasons other than cold. 'You can go back to Miss Fellowes now,' she said, crossing her arms over her chest.

'I would rather not.'

'Then why were you kissing her?' It was childish to ask such questions. She should at least have the sense to pretend it had never happened.

'She was kissing me,' he said.

'It is near to the same thing.'

'I beg to differ,' he said. 'There is the matter of consent to be considered.'

'I suppose she forced herself upon you,' Lily said sceptically.

'It was a surprise attack,' he replied.

'Well, whatever it was, you do not need to explain it away,' she said. 'It does not matter to me what you do.'

'Then why are you crying?'

'I am not.' She swallowed hard, trying to stop.

The hands on her back went to her waist and he turned her around to face him. His fingertips brushed her wet check to prove her a liar.

She squeezed her eyes shut tight, trying to stop the flow of tears, but felt them still sneaking out and wetting her lashes. But if she did not look at him, at least she did not have to see the pity in his eyes. 'I was startled. That is all.' Then she added, 'I thought you had better taste.'

He chuckled. 'The next time, I shall find someone worthy of your approval.'

'The next time...' Before she could argue that she had no intention of passing judgements on his inamorata, his lips touched hers. Then they were gone again.

'I meant, the next time it will be you,' he said with a smile. 'I was looking for you. I heard singing and I thought, perhaps...' He paused. 'Do you sing?'

She frowned. 'Would you like me to?'

Now he looked like his embarrassed younger self. 'I don't require it of you, if that's what you're asking. But I still know very little about you and what you do for pleasure.'

'I can sing, but I seldom have reason to,' she said.

'That is a shame.' A curl had come loose from its pin and he twisted it around his finger before brushing it off her face. 'While I cannot assure you that my return will have you singing for joy, I can promise that there will be no more tears over the kind of foolishness you witnessed just now in the trophy room. Now that I am finally home, I have no wish to take up with another. Let us put the past behind us. As long as you are loyal to me, I shall be loyal to only you.'

It sounded suspiciously like he was forgiving her for having Stewart. There was a nagging doubt at the back of her mind arguing that, since she had not been at fault, there was really no reason for forgiveness. But her heart leapt at the chance for a fresh start with the man she had adored from afar.

She nodded.

'Very good,' he said, the confidence returning to his smile.

Was that settled, then? If he had nothing further to say, would he leave her and go back downstairs? Suddenly, it seemed urgent that he did not. 'Why were you looking for me?' she blurted into the awkward silence.

'To give you this,' he said and kissed her again.

'Oh,' she said with a sigh. She could not help it. She was leaning into him, her mouth open, as if he had touched a sweet to her tongue, only to pull it away. She wanted more.

'But now that I have you half out of your clothes and behind a locked door, I have an even better idea,' he said, pushing the strap of her chemise to the side so he might place another kiss on the bare skin of her shoulder.

He meant *the act*. Now that the time had finally come, she didn't dare refuse. But it was broad daylight. He would see the marks that childbirth had left on her body and be disappointed. Worse yet, he would see if she was afraid, or if it hurt. God forbid, what if she did not like it at all? What if it was as bad as the last time? Everything would be so much easier to hide under the covers and after dark.

'I do not think...' she said, before another kiss stopped her words. Dear Lord, but it was good. She had never known how lonely she had been until he'd kissed her. It was as if a part of her that had been missing was restored.

'That's right,' he said into her ear. 'Do not think. Just feel.' He was undoing the laces at the back of her stays with short, efficient jerks of his fingers. Now he was lifting the garment out of the way, dropping it to the floor with one hand as her breast dropped into the palm of his other hand like falling fruit. His thumb was rubbing back and forth across the nipple, making it stand proud beneath the thin cloth of her shift.

His head dipped and he took the other one into his mouth, sucking till the wet linen clung to her body. She could feel the slight unevenness of his front teeth, rough against her, teasing but not marking. How much better would it be if her breasts were bare? And suppose he buried his face deep between her legs?

At the thought, she let out a strange, hiccupping gasp, which made him stop and smile up at her expectantly.

She shook her head, unsure of what response was expected.

He nodded in satisfaction as if he understood her without words. Then he straightened and she opened her mouth to receive another kiss.

When his lips touched hers, she was reborn. It was as if she had spent years under water, only to burst to the surface and take her first clean breath. His kiss was life for her. They belonged together, the two of them connected by breath and taste and murmured words. The thought glowed in her brain, warmed her heart and heated her blood until a tingling rush seemed to chase through her limbs and settle in a dangerous hum of arousal between her legs. Was he feeling this, as well? Or were men always inflamed, as they seemed to be?

As if to show her, his arms tightened about her, his hand spreading over the small of her back to stroke downwards, pressing her close. Then he pulled his lips away just long enough to sigh, 'Lily,' against the shell of her ear, taking a breath as though he were inhaling a flower.

'Captain Wiscombe.'

He laughed. 'Gerald. Or Gerry.' Then he cupped her bottom and lifted her, perching her on the back of a nearby bench so her knees spread and her feet dangled. He stepped between them and pushed the hem of her chemise up to her waist.

Her physical balance was as precarious as her spirit, shifting between terror and elation as the inevitable end of this journey approached. She closed her eyes. The past was the past. When the moment came, she could let herself fall and trust that he would catch her.

She was rocking on the edge of her seat and the heads of the studs that held the upholstery in its place were making ridges on the backs of her legs. From now on, when she looked at this bench, she would blush and remember the strange and primal feel of the metal branding her thighs.

He knew what she was thinking. She could see it in his smile. And now he meant to take her, not silently in a bed in the dark tonight, but right here, standing up in the daytime. His hand moved to his trousers, undoing buttons.

'Gerry,' she said on a gasp.

'Lily,' he challenged, dropping the flap of his pants and touching his body to hers, as gentle as a kiss.

For a moment, he stared down, transfixed by the sight of their bodies together. Then he slipped a hand between them and ran a fingertip along her slit, spreading the moisture from back to front.

The bottom dropped out of her world as suddenly as if the chair had been pulled out from under her. What was this feeling? Nothing in her life had prepared her for it. He pushed into her and it was even better. The slide of flesh against flesh: large, smooth and rock-hard against soft, wet, throbbing.

She gripped his forearms to steady herself as he withdrew and stroked again. This was not frightening. This was right, just as the time before had been wrong. She had promised herself to this man for this very purpose, for ever until death. But what heaven that came after could ever compare to what was happening right now?

'Gerry.' She loved the sound of his name and the taste of him on her tongue. She kissed his funny, crooked smile. She kissed the cleft in his chin and the stubble that was coming in on his throat. A moment ago, she had been afraid to do more than tug at his sleeve. But now, she dug her fingers into the side of his waist, trying to pull him closer. She was clinging to him, lost in the feel of his arms about her.

Another spasm of pleasure shook her, leaving her hungry for the movement. Without thinking, she pumped her legs as if she was on a garden swing, trying to go higher. And higher. When he answered her movements with faster, deeper thrusts, she slid her thighs up his body to his waist and locked her feet at the small of his back to hold him. Then she pumped and thrust, eager to meet each stroke, letting the speed build until she broke through the clouds, soaring like she had wings. This time, when she cried out his name it was from the explosion of joy at being so touched by such a man.

He answered with an equally explosive curse.

A joyful swearing, if such a thing was even possible. His mouth was pressed to the skin of her throat like a wild animal ready to rip the life out of her. Instead, it was as if a lion had taken her, frightened her to the core and then playfully licked to show how utterly he possessed her.

She took in a great gasp of air and giggled. There was a man inside her, a thing she had hoped never to feel again, for it meant she was helpless, trapped. But this was different. This was happiness and freedom, and when she looked into his face she saw the surprisingly sweet boy who had proposed to her, hidden inside the conquering hero.

She pushed playfully against his arm. But when he made to step away and part from her, she locked her legs just as tightly around his body to settle her opening at the root of his sex.

'Why, Mrs Wiscombe,' he said with a sigh of pleasure, 'I think you are one of those women.'

'What women are those?' She frowned back at him.

'The sort that appear all helpless only to try

to ensnare a man into an erotic adventure in the middle of the afternoon.'

She remembered Miss Fellowes in the hall and tried to pull away from him in earnest. 'I am no such thing. If that is what you are seeking, you can go right back down the stairs to that...that...'

'Only a madman would trade his fondest dream for such common coin.'

'Your fondest dream?' she asked, surprised.

'To take you hard and fast until you screamed my name,' he said, seeming quite satisfied with himself. He reached to the neckline of her chemise and gave a sudden tug, ripping the fabric to expose her breasts. He palmed one of them, rolling the nipple between his fingers. 'And I've a good mind to do it again.'

'Perhaps, on the bed,' she suggested.

'Oh, no, love. I mean to christen each piece of furniture in this room and the next.' He pushed the scraps of her shift to the side, tracing a line from throat to navel. 'Did I not say that I meant to have you any way I could think of and as often as I like?'

The words that had frightened her yesterday now made her dizzy with excitement. 'Even in the afternoon, Gerald?' she said, pretending to be shocked.

'Especially in the afternoon, Lillian,' he said, undoing his neckcloth and smiling.

Chapter Twelve

When Lily returned to the hall the following morning, the maids had replaced the broken vase with a fresh one. She pulled a flower from the arrangement, twirled it in her fingers and smiled. The blooms were open wider this morning than they had been when she'd brought them in from the garden. She was like the flowers. It had been winter for so long. But now Gerry was here, it was full summer and she had bloomed.

As he had promised, by the time they retired to the bed, they were far too tired to make love there. They had lain, dozing in each other's arms. Just before sleep had taken them, he had whispered that this was just the beginning.

They'd woken, still tired to the bone and aching in strange places. She'd rubbed his back.

He'd offered to return the favour and slipped his hand between her legs. An hour later and half a house away from him, and she was still laughing.

'We missed you at supper, Lillian.'

Her smile faltered. She replaced the flower in the vase and turned to face her brother. 'It was the headache again. I did not feel well enough to come down.'

'Nor did the captain,' her brother said with a dry smile. He reached out and touched her cheek. 'You look well enough this morning. Almost too healthy, one might say.' By the look in his eyes, he knew exactly what she had been doing, to the last prurient detail.

She stepped back, out of his reach. 'Is it possible to be too healthy?'

'Yes. If it causes you to think only of yourself and forget those around you. How is Stewart this morning?'

She could not answer the question. She had not seen him since yesterday. She had not said good-night to him. Nor had she visited with him at breakfast. In the course of a few hours, she had forgotten all about him and neglected her responsibilities as a mother. Her newfound happiness evaporated as fast as it had arrived.

Her brother nodded, reading the answer in her expression. 'I warned you yesterday that disloyalty on your part might lead to unfortunate revelations.'

'You do not need to drag him into this,' she said. 'I said nothing more to Gerald about your plans.'

'Nothing more.' Ronald frowned at her. 'Which means that you did as much damage as you could before I could speak to you.'

'You are putting me in an impossible position,' she said, holding her hands out to him in supplication. 'He is my husband. I cannot refuse him and I should not deceive him. If you wish to keep secrets from him, then do not include me in your plans.'

Now Ronald smiled again. 'My thoughts exactly.' Then he said nothing. The silence was more ominous than his threats had been, for it meant that there was something in the works to settle with Gerry and there was no way to warn him about it.

Ronald made a little shooing gesture. 'Do not

stand there gawping at me, Lillian. You told me not to speak. I am giving you what you asked for. Now go to your little boy and explain your everlasting devotion to a man who could never want him.'

She did as he suggested and hurried to the nursery so she might prove her brother wrong. Balancing her husband and her child would be difficult, for a time. But it was nothing that all the other wives and mothers did not do. It might be unfamiliar to her, but it would not take long to learn.

She would begin by reassuring Stewart that the captain's return had changed nothing between them. He must not think he was being replaced in her heart by a man who did not love or understand him.

And surely that misunderstanding was a temporary thing. Two days at home had done much to dissipate her husband's anger over what had happened in his absence. In a week, or perhaps two, they could revisit the subject of Stewart's future and she would persuade Captain Wiscombe to relent.

Gerald.

She sighed. After last night, he was Gerald. Or Gerry, as he wished to be called. She smiled. She would very much enjoy changing his mind.

When she arrived at the nursery, Miss Fisher, the governess, met her at the door.

'How is he?' Lily whispered.

'We had a difficult night,' the servant admitted. 'He asked about you.' There was no judgement in her voice, but Lily felt it all the same.

'I am here now,' she said, smoothing her skirt and hurrying into the room.

Stewart was still at the breakfast table, poking a toast soldier into his egg as if he wished to drown it. He glared up at her.

She ignored his mood and stepped forward to kiss him on the cheek. 'Good morning, darling. Did you sleep well?'

'No,' Stewart said and went back to stabbing his egg.

'I am sorry that I did not come to kiss you good-night,' she said, and smiled. 'You will have to take two kisses from me this morning.'

'You were with him,' Stewart accused, not looking up.

'He is...' She had been about to say, *your fa-*

ther. Was there any point in adding to the lies? 'The captain has been away for a very long time. I must spend some time with him, even if it means that I cannot come to you as often as I did.'

'When he sends me to school, you won't have to see me at all.' He crushed his toast against the plate.

'Stewart.' How could she comfort him when his worst fear was exactly what Gerald planned for him? 'Stewart.' She knelt down beside his chair and put her arms around him. 'I know you are afraid that things are changing. But I am your mother and I love you more with each day that passes. And I would never make you go anywhere that you do not want to go.' Her throat tightened with what felt like the beginning of tears. She pulled him close so he could not see the wetness on her lashes and held until she felt the resistance leave his body and he hugged her back.

When she pulled away, she could smile again. 'Tell Miss Fisher there will be no lessons today. To make up for last night, I will spend extra time with you this morning. You are my boy. My miracle. Nothing will change that.'

'Papa will,' Stewart said, still not smiling. 'He will change everything.'

Chapter Thirteen

A duel.

When he'd returned to his room after a delightful night in his wife's bed, Gerry had noticed the letter slipped under his bedroom door, and assumed it was another note from the boy. He'd sat down on the trunk of clothes that had been delivered from London, opened it and scanned the note in his hand. Then he'd read it again, more slowly, sure that it had to be a badly worded joke.

Captain Wiscombe,
Yesterday afternoon, I witnessed you kissing Miss Fellowes in the trophy room. For the offence to my honour, and the honour of the lady in question, I challenge you to meet me, tomorrow morning, at dawn. My second, Mr Ronald North...

Aha. It was serious. And there was the true instigator of the thing. Ronald had convinced the Fellowes woman that a meeting would be welcome. Then he had put the baronet up to taking action. And Gerry could think of no man in England who was less capable of action than Chauncey d'Art.

A man of violence would have stormed into the trophy room and stopped the kiss. He would have issued the challenge face to face, perhaps after a sharp punch to the offender's jaw. At the very least, he would have put the lady's honour ahead of his own in this pathetic letter.

Sir Chauncey was an utter failure at being a man. And now Gerry was going to have to shoot him, which would ruin his perfect morning. Where was he to find a second? He did not even have a valet, much less a local friend who would want to end a seven-year separation by getting up before dawn and loading a pistol.

He crumpled the paper and tossed it aside, undoing the latches on the trunk and searching for clean linen and a coat suitable for another man's funeral.

Of course, he must not let it come to that.

Gerry hated duelling almost as much as he did hunting. It was not that he was incapable of either, or doubted his inevitable success. He simply did not see the sport in killing just to prove his manhood. There were times when diplomacy was a better answer than war. The fact that he had no experience with peace did not mean he could not wage it.

Once properly washed, shaved and dressed, he walked down the hall to the guest wing and rapped sharply on the door of Sir Chauncey's bedroom. Then he entered without waiting for an invitation.

The poor man sat on the edge of the bed. At Gerry's interruption, he stood unsteadily, hand clutching the bedpost for support. He was wearing the same rumpled clothes he'd had on the previous afternoon and appeared to have been drinking, or crying. Or both. He gestured at the door with his free hand. 'You cannot...'

'It is my house,' Gerry said. 'I think I can.'

Sir Chauncey tried again. 'You are not to see me until the duel. It is bad luck.'

'I believe you are thinking of brides and

grooms and weddings,' Gerry said as patiently as possible, shutting the door behind him to prevent Ronald North from appearing out of nowhere to offer help where none was needed. 'Since an effort should be made to reconcile differences before resorting to violence, there is no reason we should not talk.' He pulled a chair from the fireside and placed it next to the bed, then gestured for the baronet to sit again.

Sir Chauncey sank back on the mattress as obedient as a dog. 'We cannot settle this by talking. You have humiliated me by seducing my fiancée.'

Gerry sighed. 'I do not know which part of that statement is more ludicrous. First, I was not the instigator. She set upon me in the trophy room. Secondly, there was no seduction. I managed to escape before I was as mounted as the rest of the animals in there. Thirdly, she is not your fiancée, she is your mistress. It is you who should be apologising to me for bringing her to my house.'

'I know what I saw.' Sir Chauncey raised an accusing finger. It trembled slightly, spoiling the effect.

Gerry grinned. 'You saw it, did you? Then unless you ran like a frightened girl, you saw my wife interrupt the kiss seconds after it began. I went to comfort her and spent the rest of the day in her bed, apologising.' Not in bed, precisely. But there was a limit to honesty and that crossed it.

'I know the two of you were in the trophy room. I saw you both enter. And later, she was not at dinner,' he said petulantly.

'Who else was missing?' Gerry asked.

'Ronald North was late,' he admitted in a sullen voice.

'And I suppose he was the one that alerted you to this supposed tryst and suggested the duel,' Gerry said.

There was a flicker of clarity on the baronet's face, before it settled back to belligerence. 'Someone must pay for this slight to my honour.'

'Do you mean to shoot Ronald North, once you have finished with me? I will not allow that, either.'

'What would you have me do?' said Sir Chauncey, annoyed.

Gerry leaned forward to speak confidentially.

'Let me tell you how this will end, if we continue on the course you have set. If we fight, I will kill you. Then I will have to flee the country to escape the scandal.'

Sir Chauncey went white at the mention of his probable fate.

Gerry ignored it. 'I would not enjoy it, of course.'

'Killing me?'

'No. Fleeing the country.' Gerry sighed. 'I cannot abide travel, I am thoroughly tired of the Continent. I am just beginning to enjoy my home and do not want to leave it.' The truth of that statement was almost as big a surprise as the letter of challenge. He enjoyed his house. He enjoyed his wife. Only a few things stood between him and a perfect life.

He looked back at Sir Chauncey, annoyed.

'I might win,' Sir Chauncey said, hopefully.

Gerry shook his head. 'That might be what Ronald was hoping, when he orchestrated this fiasco. But it is an impossibility. I might simply wound you, which will hurt very much. And with even the smallest wound, there is the risk of sepsis, protracted suffering and death. If a single thread from your shirt is driven into your body by the ball and not removed?' He released a puff of air and gestured to express the escaping soul.

Sir Chauncey went even paler.

Gerry nodded in sympathy. 'I would not want you to suffer. More likely, I will kill you quickly and flee. Then Ronald will keep both my house and your mistress. You may not have noticed, but the Norths are very good at separating people from their valuables.' Then he smiled and shrugged, as if to say, *Family. What are we to do with them?*

At this, Sir Chauncey looked depressed. 'There is no hope for me, then.'

Gerry patted him on the back. 'Of course there is, my dear man. First, you must accept my apology for any pain or dishonour I've caused you. And I am sorry, truly. Once we are settled, I suggest you call for your carriage, immediately. Tell Ronald that you have seen through his devious plan and want no part in it. Then leave.' It took an effort not to smile at his own suggestion. 'Take Miss Fellowes with you. And tell her that if there is any more nonsense you will end your arrangement with her.'

'Will that work, do you think?' Sir Chauncey brightened.

Gerry leaned forward and clapped him on the shoulder. 'Damn it, man. Of course it will work. You are a baronet, not some nobody. If she prefers another to you, then leave her at the first inn you pass and make her fend for herself. There are dozens of women who are just as pretty and will not have their heads turned by the first redcoat they see.' He stood to go.

Sir Chauncey stood as well and took his hand. 'You are right, Captain. I must assert myself.'

'You must and you will, Sir Chauncey. I have every confidence in you. And, if I do not see you before you go, farewell, Sir Chauncey.'

'Au revoir,' Sir Chauncey said.

'Farewell,' Gerry said, more firmly, and let himself out of the room. Then he went to tell Mrs Fitz that there would be two less at supper.

Lily walked quickly down the hall on the main floor, stopping in the open trophy room door to clap her hands. After a moment's pause to listen for Stewart's faint answering clap, she moved down the hall to the billiard room. Since the remaining guests were out for a morning hunt and her husband was still resting in his room, she had promised Stewart the run of the house and a spirited game of hide-and-seek. But the boy knew the house so well that without the help of clapped clues, it was impossible to find him.

She opened the billiard room door suddenly, hoping to catch him unawares. Her cry of 'Ha!' was premature. The room was dark and empty. Back to the trophy room, and the library beyond it.

She moved quickly through the cases of stuffed birds and over the bearskins on the floor, trying to ignore the glass eyes staring down from the walls. Even after seven years, the room made her uncomfortable. Perhaps, when the guests were gone, Gerry would banish the last of the animals and find a better use for the space they occupied.

But today she could hear Stewart's voice from the adjoining library. He was speaking to someone, answering questions pitched too low to carry to the next room. Could it be Gerry? She smiled in anticipation. If her husband would just take the time to talk to the boy, he might see there would be no harm in Stewart's remaining at the Chase.

She opened the door to surprise them and her smile faded.

'And how old are you now, boy?' The Earl of Greywall was lounging against a library table, his hand resting on Stewart's shoulder.

For a moment, she was too shocked to say anything at all. She took great pains to keep her son away from the guests and made sure that he had no part in the schemes of his grandfather and uncle. He was so good at staying out of sight that many of the visitors had come and gone totally unaware that a little boy had shared the house with them.

She'd made it especially clear that he was not to bother the earl, informing the boy that he was a very important man with no time for children. It gave the peer far too much credit, but Stewart had been convinced. But now he had been trapped, just as she was. The headache which had been gone for nearly two days returned with a vengeance.

Greywall looked up at her and smiled, his question forgotten. 'Your son, I presume?'

'And Captain Wiscombe's,' she replied, pulling Stewart away from the earl and to her side.

'We were just talking.' The earl's smile became a leer. 'Since you refuse to speak at dinner, I must find others to converse with.'

'Children are better seen than heard,' she said, hoping that Stewart understood the warning. Then she took a few carefully controlled breaths and forced herself to do something she'd not done in ages. She smiled at the Earl of Greywall. 'And I must make an effort to be better company.' Her stomach churned at the thought. But for the moment, nothing was more important than getting Stewart out of the room and away from this man.

'Perhaps, if I ask the captain, he will allow the boy to join us for a hunt.'

'I do not like hunting,' the boy said and Lily felt the muscles under her fingers go rigid.

'Nonsense,' responded the earl. 'You are old enough, I am sure. Tell me, boy, when were you born?'

'I will decide when he is old enough to hunt,' Lily snapped, before Stewart could answer, pulling him closer. 'Or his father, the captain, shall.'

'Mama, you are holding me too tight,' he whispered, squirming to get away from her.

'Yes, Lillian,' the earl said. 'Let the boy go. You cannot protect him for ever.' He was smiling at Stewart again, leaning close enough to him that Lily could smell the brandy mingling with his foul breath. She had to go. If she did not leave immediately, she would be sick. But she could not leave without her son.

The earl leaned even closer and reached out a hand. 'And he is a fine, handsome lad. Just like his father.'

'Thank you.' Gerry was standing in the doorway, his hand resting on the frame. He stared at the three of them, face expressionless, though she was sure his eyes missed no detail.

Without bothering to explain, she seized Stewart by the arm and pulled him from the room, hurrying him through the trophy room and down the hall without looking back.

Chapter Fourteen

'The party is somewhat diminished tonight,' Gerry said, nodding at the empty places up and down the supper table.

Lily gazed back at him, forcing her expression into a placid smile. She had not spoken to her husband since he had discovered her in the library with the earl. In the silence of her bedroom, she'd gone through the conversation again and again, trying to decide what her husband might have seen or heard. What had he read into the few shared words? They had been ordinary enough.

But Gerry was perceptive, almost too sharp for his own good. The empty chairs at the table tonight were proof of that. They had both been too busy to notice the departure of the Wilsons yesterday. After seeing the dyed stoats that might have been their future, they had waited only long enough for the skies to clear before setting off for London.

Today, the baronet and his Cyprian had set off as well. She was sure that it was Gerry's doing, but she was almost afraid to ask how he had managed it. Perhaps he would evict Greywall as well, without requiring an explanation for the afternoon's exchange. Then the Burkes would go and they would have the house to themselves.

'We are no less jovial for the smaller numbers,' her father said with a smile, reminding her that ridding themselves of the guests would not be enough to set her free.

'It will give us the opportunity to better know our host,' said Mrs Burke, obviously pleased that a lack of competition had finally gained her a seat near the head of the table.

'Yes, it will. I find I am most eager to speak with him,' Greywall said and Lily reached for her wine to hide her apprehension.

'You flatter me, madam,' Gerry replied to Mrs Burke. The earl's lips barely moved as he spoke and the sound of his voice did not carry to the others at the table. It was meant just for her, as a reminder that their talk in the library had been innocent in comparison with the one he could have with Gerry.

She must make sure that it did not happen. Her husband was in an excellent mood this evening. She would do her best to keep him so and to keep him away from the peer.

Or perhaps Mrs Burke would do the job for her. She was too close to him, batting her lashes and behaving as Miss Fellowes had done before her sudden departure. It would have annoyed her had Gerry not shot her a look that hinted the hero of Salamanca wished to be rescued from his own dinner table.

She would ignore Mrs Burke, and the earl, as well. She smiled at him, as if his words were polite dinner conversation and not threat. Then she went back to her meal. Only a few more days, she assured herself. He would be gone and he would not be coming back.

'Flatter you. Captain?' The conversation at the other end of the table continued and Mrs Burke was as loud as the earl was quiet. 'It is nothing but truth. I've often said to Mr Burke that it would be fascinating to speak to a great hero like Captain Wiscombe.' She planted a meaty hand on Gerry's arm and gave an affectionate squeeze. Her own husband, who sat on Gerry's opposite side, seemed surprised to be included in the discussion and offered an ambivalent nod.

Gerry shook his head. 'I am no storyteller, madam. But I look forward to a quiet evening in the company of you and your husband. I would not mind a few hands of cards after dinner, if any of you are so disposed.' He was using the same cheerfully innocuous tone he'd employed since he'd returned. As usual, there was an iron resolve behind it that put Lily on her guard.

'My God, yes,' the earl said, draining his glass again and looking up the table. 'It is about time that someone with money in their pockets joins us. I am tired of losing. Let it be Wiscombe's turn.'

'Yes,' Ronald said. 'By all means, join us.' He was almost salivating at the prospect of a game.

Which meant that her brother would attempt to cheat him as he had everyone else who played. The warnings she had given him had done no good. She glared at her father, willing him to understand the danger that such a game might create.

'Are you sure you might not prefer billiards?' her father suggested. But he was putting none of his usual effort into guiding the conversation to suit his ends. Perhaps, in the end, he cared no more for Ronald than he did for her.

'No,' Gerry said firmly. 'Tonight it must be cards. I am feeling lucky. We will all play cards.' He stared down the table to her and raised his glass in a private salute.

After the stress of the afternoon, she longed to retire to her room and avoid the impending doom. But the glance Gerry had given her was as clear as a verbal command. She was to attend him and the guests. She answered with a barely perceptible nod.

When dinner was finished, they retired to the sitting room and pushed two tables together so all seven of them could play. Lily held her breath as Gerry took his seat opposite her brother at the card table for a round of Trade and Barter. With the speed of play and a chance to force cards when other players drew from one's hand, there were numerous opportunities to cheat. And though the earl and the Burkes had full glasses, Gerry had refused another drink after dinner. Her husband would be far too clear-headed to fall for her brother's usual tricks.

The game began simply enough, with Gerry shuffling and dealing out three cards to each of the players. After a round of spirited play, Mrs Burke took the pot with three tens. The next two hands were equally free of mischief. But such games always began innocently. It did not do to have the guests losing on the very first go. It was only when the deal turned to her brother that things would begin to go wrong.

One did not last long in the North family if one was not able, on some rudimentary level, to count cards as a game was played. By the time Ronald had finished dealing, Lily could see that there were now five aces in play.

If her husband noticed the fact, there was no indication of it. Unless she was to count the slight lift of his eyebrow as the hand was played out to Ronald's obvious success. When the deal returned to her husband, she watched as he deftly palmed the second ace of hearts and dropped it to the floor at her brother's feet. Play continued as it had, with the addition of a slight frown on her brother's face as he realised that the card he needed was no longer in the deck.

When the hands were revealed, Mr Burke was the one to take the pot. And the next as well, when he was the dealer. It appeared to Lily that her husband went out of his way to lose, when he could control the play at all. He was displaying an ineptitude that would have had any in her family gloating at their inevitable success.

But there had been the matter of that ace. And now the deal had returned to her brother. When he had finished, his hand had four cards, not three, and he was careless in disguising the fact. When cards were exchanged, he retrieved the ace he'd dealt to Father, forced an unwanted deuce on the earl and slipped the spare card he'd drawn back up his sleeve. Then he knocked on the table to stop play and displayed his three aces, reaching for the pot.

'Damnable good luck you have, North,' Mr

Burke said, mopping his forehead with a hand-kerchief.

'He makes his own luck,' Gerry said, 'because he cheats at cards.' The pronouncement was delivered in the same tone he might have used had he been remarking on the weather.

There was an audible gasp from the people at the table. All except for Lily, since she could not even manage to pretend surprise.

'I beg your pardon?' Though his voice was calm, Ronald's face was white with rage.

Gerry held a hand to his ear. 'Was that an apology? If so, it was not very convincing.'

'It is no such thing. I have nothing to apologise for.' Her brother pushed back his chair as if a few inches of distance would be enough to escape the allegation.

Gerry reached beneath the table and grabbed the fifth ace, dropping it in the centre for all to see.

At this, Mr Burke tossed his cards on the table in disgust. Even the impervious Greywall let out a curse.

'You cannot prove that was mine,' Ronald said, trying to salvage the situation.

'Perhaps not.' Gerry grabbed her brother by the wrist and forced his hand, palm up, on the table, revealing the king of clubs that was hidden in his shirt cuff. 'But this did not appear by magic.' Then he flipped up the remaining cards in the deck and fanned them to show the tidy stack of face cards arranged at the bottom. 'And I think it unlikely that this is a coincidence.'

'I am sure this is just an innocent mistake,' her father said, offering a smile so benevolent that the look in Mr Burke's eyes changed from suspicion to confusion.

'Unfortunately, no.' Gerry was unmoved. 'There is nothing innocent about what is happening here.'

'Of course there isn't,' Ronald announced. 'It is clear that Captain Wiscombe wishes to defame me and has created evidence where none existed. The person to make such accusations often does it to conceal their own guilt.'

Lily balled her fists under the table to prevent herself from speaking. It was bad enough that

Ronald had been caught. He'd made it worse by arguing. Now that he'd accused Gerry of dishonour, the end was inevitable.

There was a dangerous pause before her husband spoke. 'Ronald North, you have been defrauding the visitors to my house. Since you are my wife's brother, I will ignore the aspersions on my character. But I demand you apologise to my guests and make immediate recompense for any money you have taken from Mr Burke.' He paused, as if the next words pained him. 'And Lord Greywall also.'

Lily held her breath and prayed that Ronald might display, if not honour, than at least common sense. His position was hopeless. He must give in.

'There is nothing to apologise for. If it is not you, then someone else has played a prank on me.' He glared at the people around the table, waiting for someone to come to his defence.

It was hopeless. He lacked their father's charm. When he was cornered he could not turn the opinion of the room back to his favour.

Gerry sighed. 'No one is tricking you. You are the trickster. If you do not care to admit it, then I must teach you some manners. We will begin with the correct way to issue a challenge. It is done thusly—face-to-face and eye to eye, not with a letter slipped under a door. Ronald North, you have insulted me and cheated the guests in my home. Apologise now or meet me on the field of honour to take your punishment.'

Chapter Fifteen

The room was in uproar. Mrs Burke was shriek-
ing and her husband pushed away from the table
so fast he upset it, sending the cards spilling to
the floor. The elder North was entreating for
reason and calm. The earl simply laughed. The
sound was long and bitter, and punctuated by
demands for more drink.

Ronald North was swearing under his breath.
By the look in his eyes, he would be only too
happy to shoot Gerry right now, if only for the
chance to make up for his ruined evening.

Gerry smiled back at him. It was another proof
that the man did not think through his actions,
or he'd have realised what a mistake he'd made.
Everyone in the room should have had the sense
to see this moment coming. Instead, they were

demonstrating their stupidity with this display of shock and horror. He felt almost sorry for them.

Almost. But not quite.

The one voice he did not hear was his wife's. When he turned to look for her, she was already gone. While he had not expected her to share his feelings of triumph, he had hoped that she would at least remain long enough to act surprised by the turn of events, as her father was. Ronald had to be punished. If she did not want her reputation to be tainted with his bad behaviour, she needed to be seen at her husband's side.

Now Mrs Burke was asking about her. Gerry muttered something about a megrim and overwrought nerves, then offered to summon the woman's maid so that she might be escorted to her room, as well. It gave him reason to quit the sitting room and leave the chaos behind him to locate Lily.

Her sudden absence filled him with an unease that he'd not experienced since the war. Things had been going better than he could have imagined. The previous afternoon, her devastation on witnessing a single kiss had assured him that no matter what had gone before, he now held her heart in the palm of his hand. Then she had demonstrated her devotion in the sweetest possible way. His body tightened at the memory.

But that was yesterday. What with the nonsense over Sir Chauncey, he'd had no time to tell her of his plans for her brother. Despite the fact that the man was a bounder, he was still blood to her. She'd deserved some kind of warning about how the evening might end.

And he had yet to enquire about the curious scene he'd interrupted in the library. The Greywall he knew cared for nothing but hunting and wine. This sudden interest in his wife's son could not be good. Perhaps he had guessed the boy's illegitimacy and meant to blackmail Lily into extending his invitation.

It had been a spontaneous act of chivalry to step in and claim the boy as his own. Now he would have to explain to Lily that there had been no change in his plans for the boy's future. It was much easier to lie to Greywall than to lie to himself. The boy was not his and there was no way to forget that.

When he reached his bedroom, she was waiting for him, wearing the same prim gown she'd worn on the first night. Her face had no trace of powder and her red-brown hair was down, tied back from her face with a ribbon. His heart caught in his chest. How could he ever be worthy of such a beauty?

Perhaps she was thinking the same thing. The smile she wore was the same cold and distant look she used on her unwelcome guests. Perhaps the previous night's affection had been an act and she was more of a North than he wanted to believe. Or perhaps he had created this distance himself.

He returned her cold smile with a warm one and sat on the edge of the bed to pull off his boots. If the current displeasure related to what had just occurred in the sitting room, it would be better to get it out in the open immediately. 'Well, it looks like I shall have to shoot your brother.'

From behind him, there was silence.

He cursed himself for his ham-handedness. Trying to make a joke out of a life-and-death matter might have worked on the battlefield, where all men behaved as if they were one step from the grave, but it was foolhardy of him to try such cruel tactics on his wife.

He was one breath from apologising when she replied, 'Someone was going to do it eventually.'

Her response seemed just as flip as his greeting and showed no sympathy for the difficult position he was in. 'He was cheating at cards,' Gerry repeated the obvious. 'I caught him in the act.'

'Of course you did,' Lily answered. 'He is not nearly as good at it as he thinks.'

'I could not just let it stand,' he said, pulling off his neckcloth and walking to the wardrobe to remove the rest of his clothes. He could feel her eyes boring holes in his back, but did not turn. What would the world think if it learned that the hero of Salamanca was afraid to look his own wife in the face?

'Will the duel be tomorrow? Or will there be more time?' she asked.

'At least a day, I think. There are formalities. We must choose seconds, a location and weapons.' When he had nothing left to remove but his shirt, he turned to look at her, braced for whatever storm of emotion might come.

'Being honourable is surprisingly complicated,' she said, the corner of her mouth lifting
in an ironic grimace.

'Not really.' He frowned. She was carrying
it too far if she thought that the honour of his
household was a joking matter. 'It is not the least
bit complicated. Most men understand that it
is wrong to cheat at cards, sharp at billiards or
trick men out of their houses so they might use
the land to swindle others.'

'We Norths do not know any other way. But
I will take you at your word.' Now the irony
turned to bitter sarcasm.

'You are a North now, are you?' he said, hands
on hips.

'I am a Wiscombe,' she said. 'Or at least I
thought I was.'

'I am sorry that I did not give you warning of
what I meant to do,' he said, suddenly not the
least bit sorry. 'But it had to be done.'

'I know,' she all but shouted back at him. 'And
it does not matter to me what you do to him. Kill
him, for all I care. We will all be better off.'

He shook his head in disgust. 'Kill him? Duelling and going to war is no different from shoot-

ing animals to you, is it? Do you have no feelings at all, that you would turn on your own kin and ask me to butcher them?'

'Do you want me to prefer them to you?' she said, equally disgusted. 'Just what is it that you want from me?'

What did he want from her? 'I expect you to show some natural, human feeling towards your own blood.'

'Natural?' She gasped. 'And what does that mean to you? In my family, it is natural for a woman's blood to sell her to a stranger to gain a house.' She took another ragged inhalation. 'And then to forget all about her, so she might be raped by a drunkard without so much as a by your leave.' Now she was struggling for breath, clutching at her temples as if only her hands pressing against them kept her skull from splitting in two.

Perhaps there was no air in the room, for he could not seem to breathe, either. Rape. Why had he not suspected this? It explained her unreasonable fears, the panic and the megrims that were no mere sham to avoid responsibility.

He should have demanded answers when he'd

first heard of the child. Instead, he'd believed the worst and never bothered to look for the truth. Nor had it occurred to him that she might have been even more trapped by this marriage than he had been. She'd been expected to marry the nothing that he had been, a man so unworthy that he had not even bothered to speak to her before he'd proposed. Then he'd abandoned her to her fate, assuming that she would be safe until he returned.

He had been wasting time on trivialities. The only problem in this house that mattered was right here in front of him. And he'd ignored it.

He sat down beside her, seized her by the wrists and prised her hands away from her face. She was sobbing with fear and pain, so he rubbed her temples himself, urging her to lean forward until their foreheads touched, waiting for her to relax. 'It will be all right. Breathe, Lily. Just breathe.' He kept his own breath slow and steady to guide her back to composure.

It was working. She soothed at the sound of his voice and copied his breathing. The furrows in her brow began to relax and her head lolled against his shoulder. 'Thank you,' she whispered, pressing her face into his throat like a child in need of comfort. 'I am sorry to be so emotional. I know there was nothing else you could do. It is just…'

'You did nothing wrong. Ever. It was I.' He turned his face to kiss her. But even as he did it, he knew that he was that stranger she'd dreaded when she spoke of being sold. For much of the past seven years, she had kept a secret from him. His homecoming must have been a cause of fear, not a hope of salvation. Today, that would end.

He released her hands and wrapped his arms about her, nuzzling her hair. 'Tell me what happened while I was gone.' His mouth was pressed close to her ear, so he spoke in little more than a whisper.

'I thought that was obvious. I lay with another man and he left me with child.' Her brittle laugh was muffled by the linen of his shirt. 'Of course, as you said about Miss Fellowes, there is the matter of consent to consider.'

He had all but joked about being unable to fight off that woman's unwanted attentions. But Lily did not have the advantage of size and strength. She had been helpless.

'Who was he?'

She gasped and tried to pull away. 'You're hurting me.'

He cursed himself. He had been imagining what he would do when he'd found the bastard. Without thinking, he'd tightened his grip on her. Lily, of all people, deserved the gentleness she had never been offered. He forced himself to relax, rubbing the centre of her back in a way that calmed them both. 'No one will ever hurt you again. I will see to it. Now tell me what happened.'

'There is really nothing to tell,' she said. But he could feel her tremble as she gathered the nerve to speak. 'I used to spend the evenings with my father's guests, acting as a true hostess. One night, a man mistook common courtesy for something more.' Her breath caught in her throat and he put his hand on her heart, breathing with her until she could regain control.

Then he said, 'He followed you to your room?'

She shook her head. 'It was worse than that. As an honoured guest, Father gave him the master bedroom. I did not think it would matter. The other bedrooms were full and he had to stay somewhere. I locked the connecting door. But the key was in his dresser. And he assumed...'

At the first hitch in her breathing, he kissed her until she was calm again. 'He forced his way into your room.'

'Worse than that,' she whispered. 'He carried me back here. To your bed. And the animals on the walls... So many eyes...' She was crying in earnest, reliving the details.

It had been horrible enough to sleep here under the best of circumstances. But at the thought of her in his father's old room, he was gripped by the sick terror that had taken him on the night before his first battle. 'And after that, you changed the locks and the decoration,' he finished for her.

She nodded into his shoulder. 'I pushed the wardrobe in front of the connecting door until he was gone. Then I had the servants remove everything from the room and burn it.'

Apparently, she'd enjoyed that one small act of rebellion, for he felt her laugh. 'They thought I was very strange. So I told them you had not liked the room and had requested the changes.'

'Good for you,' he said, laughing in response. 'It was abominable.' The thought of using it as a bridal chamber had been one of the reasons he'd postponed his own wedding night. In the end, he'd spared her nothing.

'I had the locks changed and left the room empty for a time, claiming that I could not decide what to do with it. But then I read of your successes in the newspapers. I decided to make a space that would be worthy of you, should you ever return to me.'

She sounded so hopeful at this imagined homecoming that he felt even worse for his recent behaviour.

'As I told you before, it was just the one time,' she was assuring him, as if she still feared he still meant to blame her for what had happened. 'I learned not to be so trusting. I limited my time with the guests. It was better to appear cold than to risk another incident.'

'And your headaches?' he said.

'Sometimes the guests are too much for me to bear. My head hurts and I become short of breath. If I go to my room to rest, I am better in no time.'

'You are a prisoner in your own home,' he said,

outraged. 'You should not have to hide behind a locked door to get any peace.'

'It is not so bad,' she said hurriedly. 'It is a very nice house. And I have Stewart to care for.'

There was the boy again, a continual reminder of what had happened to her. Something must be done. But for now, it was time to put the blame for the problem back where it belonged. 'And who is Stewart's father?'

She eyed him warily. 'If I tell you, what do you mean to do?'

'I will make him pay for what he did to you. When I am finished with him, he will have no life left in his body to prey upon another innocent.'

'Before or after you fight my brother?' she said with a sigh.

It must seem that he could not solve a problem without shedding blood. He took her hand, squeezing it and pressing it to his lips. 'I will not have you blaming yourself for a thing that was not your fault. The man responsible will be brought to justice, one way or another. First, I will clear our house of guests, including your family, who should have protected you in my absence.' All her father's fine words about caring for his precious girl had had been nothing more than another trick. 'Once that is done, I will see to your attacker.'

She gave an emphatic shake of her head. 'You are too late for that. He is already dead. There is nothing to be done.'

She had spoken too quickly. But what reason would she have to lie, now that he knew the worst? 'There must be something,' he said. 'I cannot just leave this...' All the accolades and medals he'd earned meant nothing if he could not manage to care for his own wife. He was worthless and unworthy, just as his father had said.

'You have done enough just by coming home safe,' she said, lifting her head and giving him a tear-stained smile. 'It means we have a future together. But the past is the past. It is over. Leave it,' she whispered, touching his arm. 'For me.'

At that slight pressure of her hand, he felt himself break. He gathered her to him again and gave her the homecoming kiss he'd imagined when first he'd left her. She was right. The time apart did not matter. There was only now and what would come.

And if he could have this moment, it was more than enough. He could live and die on the taste of her mouth, the scrape of her tongue on his teeth and the feel of her cheek against his. 'Ask for the world and I shall get it for you,' he said.

'Not the world,' she whispered back. 'Just your trust.' She hesitated. 'And perhaps, one day, your love?'

'My trust is yours, as it always should have been.' He could not promise more than that. He'd wasted years of his life, hating the faithless seductress he was sure he'd married. But he had been wrong. The woman before him was a blameless stranger. How could he know what he truly felt for her, other than a driving need to undo his mistakes and make things right?

He kissed her again and reached to undo the buttons on her gown. He felt her tense. Yesterday, they had been in her room. But even after stripping this room to the plaster and swearing that the past did not matter, there were memories in this place that still needed to be banished.

'You can trust me,' he said and felt her force herself to relax.

He quickly pulled his own shirt over his head and cast it to the floor, making sure he was naked and vulnerable before asking the same of her. Then he placed her hands on the little pearl buttons, kissing her fingers for encouragement.

Slowly, she undid them and his eyes followed the widening vee of bare skin down to its point just above her navel. He traced the same path with his tongue, kissing her throat, nuzzling the insides of her breasts and finally resting his cheek against her stomach, dipping his tongue into her navel, licking and swirling.

She released a shuddering sigh and arched her back, as her hands caught in his hair, pressing him tighter to her. But she made no move to guide him lower.

The last time, he had been selfish. He had been so eager for her that he'd taken more than he'd given. The only other man who had touched her had been even worse. And now she had no experience to know what it was that she so clearly wanted.

He smiled against her stomach. Then very

slowly, he raised the hem of her gown to bare her for his kiss. He slid his tongue down the rise of her belly.

She tensed again, still unsure.

He halted the progress of his kisses and stroked the delta of hair with his fingertips until she spread her trembling thighs to receive his hand. She stilled with a sigh as he eased his fingers into her wet, welcoming body. She wanted him there, inside her, as if she were more comfortable with his pleasure than she was with her own.

The response was tempting, but it was not what he wanted from her. Before she could object, he dipped his head and spread her even wider, replacing his hand with his mouth.

Her body went rigid and she answered the penetration of his tongue with a primal moan. At first, it seemed she might fight against him. But then the pleasure proved too great and she raised her hips as if offering herself to him.

He accepted the gift, steadied her with his hands and feasted, delving as deeply as he could into her to mimic his fingers. But still it was not the response from her that he sought. So he withdrew and left a lingering trail of kisses until he reached the little bead of flesh that would destroy the last of her resistance.

For a moment, her breathing stopped and he almost released her, fearing it was another attack of panic. Then, she gasped in amazement, and clutched at his hair to encourage him. She was sobbing now, sweet, happy whimpers that came faster and faster with each movement of his tongue.

His body answered, growing, ready and desperate to be consumed by her. He put his own needs from his mind, focusing on the sound of her cries until they stopped. Started again. Stopped. And released in a long, satisfied sigh.

He pulled away from her and lay back on the bed, achingly hard, closed his eyes and tried to think of anything but the taste on his tongue and the smell of musk. This was his gift to her. It was all he needed. When he opened them again, she was leaning over him.

He did not have to ask if he had pleased her. Her false smile was gone and had been replaced by one so real that her very soul seemed to shine out at him from behind her eyes. He smiled back.

Without a word, she stripped the gown over

her head and dropped it beside his shirt. She was kneeling at his side, a glorious topography of soft curves, hills and valleys that he longed to explore.

But he had promised himself that her pleasure was foremost. He dragged his gaze back to her face. Her hair had come undone from its tie and framed her face in wild sherry-coloured waves. He wanted to bury his face in it and lose himself in her body.

Her eyes strayed lower, admiring his obvious need for her. Then her smile widened and she turned to straddle him, her hands on his shoulders, her damp thighs squeezing his hips.

'You don't have to,' he said, his voice breaking like a green boy's.

'Even after yesterday, you don't want to bother me?' she said, teasing his body with a rock of her hips.

'I don't want to demand more than you wish to give,' he said, trying not to think. 'I want to pleasure you.'

'Then let me have my way,' she said, touching him, stroking him and, finally, easing her body down to cover him.

Chapter Sixteen

The next morning, Lily took breakfast in her room to avoid an embarrassing meeting with her guests who, unless they were even more stupid than they appeared, must have finally come to realise that the Norths had been playing them for fools. Perhaps she was a coward for not taking her share of the responsibility for what had been going on. She had been the hostess when it happened. But Gerry had uncovered her brother's cheating. It was only fair that he help with consoling the victims.

She smiled. Gerry would not mind if she did not come down at all. Last night, he had gone from commanding hero to willing slave, pleasuring her until she couldn't think. Then she'd turned the tables and ridden him, watching triumphant as he lost control because of her. She'd had no idea that something that had once seemed so horrible could be so wonderful if it was shared with the right person.

More importantly, she had finally told him enough of the truth so he knew that she would never willingly be unfaithful to him. Perhaps it had been her imagination, but after her revelation, the suspicious shadows behind his eyes had gone and a measure of his old innocence had returned. Last night he had been a bridegroom and she had finally been a bride.

It was the beginning of the fresh start that they needed. Perhaps he did not yet love her. But when the last of the guests had departed, her love for him, and Stewart's as well, would be enough to open the last seals on his heart.

Between them, they would make sure he forgot all about vengeance for previous wrongs, or dredging up the details of an incident she wanted to forget. It did not really matter if it was for her sake or to salve his own injured pride. There would be too many risks involved in seeking justice at this late date. Some people were above the law.

Even if anyone believed her story. It was more likely that revealing the truth would end with her own humiliation, while her attacker remained untouched. Challenging such a man might end with gaol or a hangman's noose for the husband who sought to defend her honour. It simply was not worth the risk.

But there were other, more immediate problems to deal with. She had just set up her easel in the conservatory for her morning hour of painting when her brother arrived. Her father was close at his heels, scanning the hall for eavesdroppers before shutting the glass double doors behind him.

'Good morning,' she said, not looking up from her work.

'Good?' Ronald gave a derisive snort. 'Do you not understand what happened last night?'

'I was there, Ronald. Gerry caught you cheating at cards and called you out.'

'"Gerry" is it now?' Ronald's voice was growing shrill. 'He threatened to kill me and you spent another night in his bed.'

'Ronald!' her father said sharply as if he were settling a fight between children. 'Your sister's marriage is none of your affair. And I warned you to be careful with Wiscombe,' he added. 'No matter what he pretends, he is not the naive young man whom we sent to war.' Then he smiled at Lily. 'The way he handled the sable farm was really quite masterful.'

'It was,' she said, surprised that she could agree with him, even on such a small thing.

'I am so glad that you both approve of him,' Ronald snapped. 'But what is to be done about the duel?'

'Done about it?' Lily said. 'What can be done? In this case, I do not think a simple apology will be enough. Perhaps you should do as he asked. If you were to reimburse the guests and throw yourself on his mercy...'

'Me? I will not abase myself to that interloper.'

'He is not actually an interloper,' she said, putting the paint box aside. 'He is the owner of the house.'

'And you are his wife,' her father reminded her with a gentle smile. 'Perhaps if you were to intercede for your brother, we might avoid an unfortunate incident.'

'Perhaps if Ronald had learned to deal from

the bottom of the deck instead of hiding cards in his sleeve, he might not have got caught.'

'You were always better at it than he,' her father agreed.

'That is in no way a compliment,' she said, remembering that he was part of the problem and turning away from him.

'It is not my technique that needs improvement,' Ronald announced. 'It has never been a problem before.'

'You have not gambled against Gerald Wiscombe before,' Lily said, trying not to smile in triumph.

'Unless we are to count the first gamble that got us the house,' her father said with a knowing nod. 'Though it took some time, he won that back from us, as well. Then there was the matter of the sables. And I heard he bested you at billiards the first night he was home.'

Lily raised her eyebrows, impressed. Ronald was as good at billiards as he was abysmal at cards.

'Well, he will not win this time,' Ronald said.

'He has won already,' their father said with a shake of his head. 'No matter what we might do,

I suspect that word of this will get out in London and the same game will not work again. It might be best to decamp quietly and begin again elsewhere.'

'Your best suggestion is that we run away?' Ronald stared at his father, outraged.

Lily nodded. 'I doubt he will follow you, as long as you do not involve him in future ventures, or try to abuse your connection to him.'

Faced with the only logical choice, Ronald ignored it. 'Nonsense. You must go to him, Lily, and convince him to retract the challenge.'

'I?' She laughed. 'What makes you think I have any control over his actions?'

He responded with a knowing grin. 'You have more control over *Gerry* than you realise. I saw the look on his face yesterday morning. And today, as well. Now that you are sharing his bed, you can lead the man about by the nether parts if you wish to.'

Years of carefully maintained calm broke in an instant and she slapped him hard across the cheek. She would not let him make the best part of her marriage sound like something vile and sinful. 'Do not speak to me that way ever again.

Even if I could control him, I do not wish to. Especially not for your sake, Ronald. I warned you from the moment he arrived not to underestimate him. You ignored me and made this muddle. I will not turn my marriage into another North family fraud to help you out of it.'

'Now, children—' her father was giving them the benevolent smile that worked so well on people who didn't know him '—do not fight over this. I am sure Lily would be willing to put in a good word for you with her husband. But you must ask more nicely than that.'

'I will not,' she said, glaring at her brother.

'You had better,' Ronald countered. 'Or I will have the talk with your son that you did not have the nerve to.'

Her anger turned to ice-cold rage. 'If you do, I will shoot you myself.'

'Lillian!' Her father looked more hurt than shocked. 'Do not talk that way to your brother.' He turned to Ronald. 'And what is this nonsense about speaking to Stewart? What does he have to do with any of this?'

'Now that her husband has returned, your precious Lillian pretends to be a devoted wife. But

Stewart is proof that she was not always so pure. If she can use her wiles to convince her husband not to throw the little bastard out in the cold, then she can spare some influence for the rest of the family.'

'Lily?' Her normally glib father could manage nothing more than her name. He was staring at her as if he expected her to deny everything so they might all go back to ignoring the past.

'Do not dare pretend you did not know,' she said, furious that he could not manage one small moment of honesty, now that the subject had been broached.

Her father gave a confused shake of his head, refusing to believe. 'I am not pretending. I do not understand. What Ronald is claiming...' He shook his head again. 'I refuse to believe that you would do such a thing.'

'That I...' It was too much. She had to get away from them and the poison they spewed, using her, ignoring her pain and then coming to her for help when things went wrong. 'The duel will go on as planned. I will do nothing to stop it.' She stared at her brother in disgust. 'Why would I help someone who thinks so little of me and is eager to tell my son that the father he worships is not his?'

Then she turned to her father. 'And you, who knows everything that goes on in this house. Do not lie to me like you do to the guests. You put that monster in the room beside mine. I locked the door, but you gave him the key. You sold my honour twice, as if it was no more important than your imaginary ruby mine.'

For a moment, there was no sign of understanding on his face. But then the truth hit him like a lightning strike. 'My dear.' His voice was unsteady and his hands trembled as he reached out to comfort her, as if it were not years too late for that. Or did he expect her to comfort him? 'I did not know. I swear on your mother's soul, I did not know.'

Her vision was blurring, as it sometimes did when she forgot to breathe. Or perhaps it was just the tears. She slapped his hands away, took a deep breath and was relieved to feel her head clearing as the fear receded and anger returned. 'Then I do not know who I hate more, the man who took advantage of me, or the one who did not even notice it happened.' She pushed past them both, slamming through the glass doors and out into the hall.

By the time she arrived at her room, her breath was coming in desperate pants. Once she turned the key in the lock, it began to slow to normal. She planted her shoulders square against the wood, adding the weight of her body to the bolt. She was safe, she repeated the word in her mind. *Safe.*

But why had she run? There had been no physical threat. Just a few sad truths and some harsh words. Now that they had been spoken, there was no power left in them.

Gerry was right. She'd used the lock for comfort. She had thought she was locking others out. But if there was nothing on the other side of the door, she had been locking herself in.

'Lily.'

She jumped. Her husband stood in the connecting doorway, staring at her with concern. One look at her face and he was across the room, pulling her into his arms. 'What has happened?'

'Nothing,' she said, breathless. 'Nothing.'

'Liar,' he said, pulling her away from the door.

But he did not question her further, simply held her, his cheek pressed to her temple, offering his strength to her.

As if by magic, the contact banished the beginning of her headache. She sighed.

'Hmmm?' He asked all his questions with a single noise.

'Better,' she admitted. And then added, 'I was speaking with my father and brother. They upset me.'

'Command me and I will make it right,' he whispered.

She shook her head. 'That is what they wish for me to do. They were badgering me to make you call off the duel. But I will not do it. I will not instruct you, nor will I blame you for your decision,' she added.

'As you wish,' he said. 'But it is not unusual for them to involve you in their plans. Does it always upset you so?'

'This time it was different,' she admitted. 'We talked about the past. My brother taunted me with Stewart's illegitimacy. And my father...' She swallowed, trying to gain control. 'My father did not know what had happened to me.'

'You have never talked to him about this?' he asked and held her even closer.

She shook her head. 'All this time, I have hated him for letting it happen to me. And for pretending that there were no problems, letting it go on and on. I was even afraid...' She choked back a sob and took another breath. 'I thought he might have planned the whole thing.'

Gerry swore.

'I blamed him for what happened. But he did not even know,' she repeated, still baffled.

'We have spoken about you,' Gerry said. 'Perhaps he is misguided about some things. But he loves you and would never intentionally hurt you.'

'Do not be a fool.' She must not forget that her husband was one of the many gulls that her father had tricked. 'He used me to trap you and it is pure luck that things turned out as well as they did.'

'He persuaded me otherwise,' Gerry said, sounding almost as bewildered as she felt by this statement. 'I do not think he would have arranged the marriage if he had not thought we'd make a decent match.'

'He is a liar and a thief,' she said, exasperated.

'But he is also your father.' Gerry shook his head. 'He can lie about many things. But there was something…' He shrugged. 'I have not told you much of my own father, have I?'

'I know that he was a hunter,' she said, thinking of the awful heads that filled the house.

'But I was not,' Gerry said with a smile. 'I was a grave disappointment to him. He thought me soft and rather useless.'

'Then I hope he can look down from heaven and see how wrong he was,' she said, indignant.

He laughed. 'I doubt he would be satisfied. I have killed more than my share of men. But I still do not kill animals. Even now, I do not see the point of it.'

'How odd,' she said, for it was.

'But your father seems to have a very high opinion of me, despite my spoiling his plans. That may change, of course, since I mean to shoot your brother.'

Was he still trying to gauge her opinion on the duel? She was still not sure she had one. 'I doubt it,' she said. 'Just now, when he was encouraging me to talk you out of it, he spoke well of you. Mostly, he is not happy with Ronald for being stupid enough to be caught.'

'Fathers and sons,' Gerry said, shaking his head. 'There are expectations between us that can be difficult to fulfil. But daughters are a different matter entirely. When we talked after the sable incident, he told me repeatedly that he would not have promised you to me if he had not thought that we would make a good match. He described you as a jewel.'

'He said no such things to me,' she said, trying not to let the bitterness show. But when had he had the chance? She'd been so angry about what had happened that she'd hardly spoken to him since Stewart was born, even though they shared a house.

'When he chose a husband for you, he went out of his way to find you a man that was in no way like himself or your brother,' Gerry said. 'Despite what occurred, I think he hoped to give you a future very like the one you will have with me.'

'Then what happened...'

'It was never his plan, if that's what you feared.'

'But it was still his fault,' she insisted.

'True,' Gerry agreed. But there was a silence after that which made her wonder if he thought more than he said.

'Do you expect me to forgive him, just because he was not actively trying to hurt me?'

She'd meant to be sarcastic, but there was something in his expression that said that was exactly what he wished.

'After all your talk of loyalty, I cannot believe you would take his side in this.' She pulled away.

'There are no sides,' he said. It was exactly the opposite of what he'd said when he'd arrived. 'I would hope that you will forgive him and me, as well. I should not have married you and left you alone. I was as much at fault as he was. I was not here when you needed me.'

'I never blamed you.' She had been too busy worrying about what would happen when he returned.

'Then I have much to be thankful for,' he said, kissing her hair. 'And whatever you feel for him, your father will not be living under this roof much longer. Before he goes, I will speak to him about this and see that you have the apology that you seek.'

Chapter Seventeen

The Burkes had fled before supper.

Lily could hardly blame them. It must have been a shock to discover that they were not so much friends as a source of income to their hosts. That said, she suspected they must have been rather stupid to have not noticed it earlier. To most guests, even the most charming venue grew tiresome after a week of continual losses at cards and billiards. But the current group had lasted almost a fortnight before Gerry had arrived to destroy their illusions.

'I suspect it was my charming personality that drove them away,' her husband said, as they walked from the house just before dawn. The previous night's supper had been a quiet affair, eaten in their rooms, followed by an early bedtime so that he might be rested for the morning.

'Now that you have returned, it is more interesting than usual,' she admitted. 'We do not usually have naked men running through the hall or intimate examinations of small animals.'

'Or so many challenges, I hope,' he added. 'Two in a week is high, even for me.'

'Two?' She looked at him in surprise.

'Did I forget to tell you about Sir Chauncey?' He waved a hand. 'Later, perhaps. It was another unsuccessful scheme of your brother's.'

'My family did not have unsuccessful schemes until you arrived,' she said, secretly rather proud.

'Well, let us hope their string of bad luck continues.' He turned grave for a moment. 'But on the off chance it should not, I would rather that you not be here to witness it. A duel is no place for a lady.' Gerry gave her a stern look, as though that would be enough to scare her away at this point in the proceedings.

'You are quite right, Captain Wiscombe,' she said with a cross frown. 'We are only halfway to the clearing where this farce is to take place and the wet grass has ruined my best boots. Even if I turn back now, they are quite beyond repair. I might as well continue.'

He laughed. 'You are a surprisingly cold-blooded creature, Mrs Wiscombe.' He gave her a sidelong glance. 'In these circumstances, at least.'

She could not help it. She blushed. Then she touched his arm. 'If you mean to do this without a second, then someone must be there to call for a surgeon, should my brother be lucky enough to wound you.'

He gave the hand on his arm a gentle pat. 'If the earl means to stand for your brother, your father would have to accompany me. That hardly seemed appropriate. And I doubt a surgeon will be necessary. But thank you for your concern.'

Surely someone would need medical attention. Unless he did not intend to shoot Ronald. Or perhaps he meant to do such a thorough job of it that there would be no point in getting a doctor. But if Gerry were hurt, who would be there to protect him from her brother? And who would protect her from the earl? She shivered.

He glanced at her, then slipped his greatcoat from his shoulders and wrapped it around her. 'It will be warmer once the sun is full up.'

'Not as warm as it was last summer. The heat then was quite oppressive.'

'Then I am lucky to have missed it.'

They were talking about the weather. How banal. What if she lost him, after less than a week together? 'Gerald,' she said, wetting her lips.

'Lillian?' He was still smiling, mocking her serious tone.

'Please be careful,' she said, releasing a sigh.

'Still not going to plead for Ronald's life?' he said. Then he grew serious. 'After today, there is a chance that you will be sharing a bed with the man who murdered your brother.'

She thought for a moment, searching her mind for the distress that ought to be there at such a time. It saddened her that she could not find it. 'I knew that it might come to this some day. It is unfair to both of us that you are the one he will meet. But what are you to do, really? What he was doing is wrong. If he refuses to stop cheating, he must be stopped by someone else. I trust that you will be as merciful as possible in your punishment of him.'

He nodded, satisfied with her answer. 'And if, as you said before, he gets off a lucky shot?'

'You must not let that happen,' she said, surprising herself with the vehemence and lack of hesitation.

'Well, well,' he said, smiling. 'I have my answer.'

'But be wary. You already know that he cheats,' she reminded him. 'Should an opportunity present itself, he will try to trick you. You must remember that my family has no honour, even in circumstances that demand it by their very nature.'

He stopped walking and stared at her. 'There is one in your family that is honourable. I am lucky to have married her.'

'Thank you.' They stared at each other for a moment in silence. But Lily had the strangest feeling that they were still talking and that something very important had been said. Then he turned and tucked her hand into the crook of his arm and walked with her the rest of the way to the duelling site.

It was one of her favourite spots in the woods, a clearing where the bluebells in spring grew so thick that it was like walking on a scented cloud. Would it be spoiled for her next year by the blood that would be shed today?

'Wait here,' he said, directing her to an oak at the side of the clearing that was well out of the way of danger. 'I will call when it is safe for you to come forward.' Then he went to join the other two men.

Her brother and the earl were already there, pacing out the ground and checking the position of the sun. Even this early in the morning, Greywall was the worse for drink. But drunk or sober, he would be no help should Ronald try any underhanded tricks. Ronald cast a look in her direction that was as dark as her own mood. *Traitor.* He did not need to speak the words for her to see what he was thinking.

Good. Let him know which side she had chosen. It was surprising that it had taken him so long to understand.

After stumbling through a brief set of instructions, Greywall held out the pistol case so the men might choose their weapons. Ronald selected first, in a desperate grab that was not quite according to protocol.

Gerald took the remaining pistol and examined it briefly, then fired at the grass at his feet. There was a loud click and a brief flash, but no report.

This was what came of having no second. She had a mind to run to them and to demand that they put a stop to this immediately.

But Gerald did not seem overly bothered. He held it up again, cocking the hammer and running the ramrod down the barrel. Then he smiled. 'I see what the problem is. It has been incorrectly loaded. You had best check yours as well, North. We want no mistakes.' Then he took powder, patch and ball, readying the weapon with a few efficient movements and another tap of the rod.

He cocked the hammer again and looked expectantly at Ronald. 'All better.'

Her brother looked decidedly pale, for it was clear that his first plan had not worked.

Greywall was too drunk to notice what was occurring. But he knew his part well enough to position the men back to back and order them to pace off the space. Then he informed them that, on the count of three, they must raise their guns and fire.

'One.' The sound was ponderous in the quiet morning air. Lily held her breath.

'Two.' It had been only a second, but the time was going so slowly, it felt as if her lungs were going to burst. But while Gerald stood rock-still, her brother's hand twitched and began to swing upwards, into position.

He meant to shoot early and catch his opponent unprepared. She had known him to be dangerous when cornered, but to see such a despicable act and to be helpless was maddening.

'Thr...'

Her own scream mingled with the final count, as she saw her brother's pistol fully up, his finger tightening on the trigger.

But Gerald was even faster, his weapon discharging in time with her brother's.

The reports of the two weapons were so close that they might have been a single shot. They were followed by a man's curse and the sharp smell of gunpowder. She turned to her husband in terror, only to see him wiping casually at a bloody spot on his cheek.

She rushed to him, weak with relief, and threw her arms about him, searching in her sleeve for her handkerchief, wet it with her tears, and dabbed at the wound.

He grinned at her. 'Only grazed. I've had worse than this shaving without a mirror. Here now. Calm yourself, woman. This is no way for a soldier's wife to behave.' Now that it was over, he looked more embarrassed than hurt.

She reluctantly pulled away from him, and made an effort to compose herself. 'Yes, Captain Wiscombe.'

'And what about me?' her brother said, voice sharp with indignation. When she turned to look, Ronald was holding his mangled right hand in his left, the pistol dropped and forgotten on the grass next to a spatter of blood. 'Damn you, Wiscombe. Damn you to hell. Look what you have done.'

'Ruined your livelihood, I should think,' her husband drawled, uninterested. 'If you are lucky enough to regain the use of that hand, it will be some time before you can deal cards with any effectiveness. I suspect the dexterity needed to hide aces and deal from the bottom is gone for good.'

'You bastard!' Ronald made a lunge in her husband's direction, ready to grab him by the throat. The sudden movement sent another spatter of blood from his injured hand and what was apparently a fresh wave of pain as well. Ronald's next curse ended in a whimper and he went back to cradling the mess that had once been his dominant hand. 'Lily, help me.'

Lily stepped forward briskly. 'Do not be an infant, Ronald. Here.' She reached up to snatch his neckcloth from around his throat, wrapping it several times around the injury tight enough so the bleeding slowed to seepage. 'Now go back to the house and get Mrs Fitz to bandage it properly.'

'Send for a surgeon,' he moaned.

Lily sniffed in disgust. 'To what end? The ball went clean through and the housekeeper can set broken fingers and stitch as well as a doctor.'

'I need laudanum,' he moaned.

'You need to reflect on your injury and thank the Lord that Captain Wiscombe did not shoot you in your black heart. You truly deserved it.'

'Lily?' Even though he was older, the pain had reduced her brother to little more than a spoiled child who expected his sister to nurse him and make all things right.

'Go!' she said, holding up a finger towards the carriage that had brought her brother and his second the short distance from the house. 'Before I tell my husband to challenge you again for misloading his weapon. If you meant to kill him, than you should be happy that he did not end your life on principle.'

Her brother gave her an injured look, limping towards the carriage, as if the slight wound he'd received had carried to his leg. Greywall put a conciliatory hand on his shoulder, then got a better look at the blood staining his coat sleeve and fainted dead away.

Or perhaps he had passed out from intoxication. Either way, it did Lily good to see him face down in the wet grass. She turned away, back to her husband, offering him a composed smile as he held out his arm to escort her.

'There,' he said. 'Did I not tell you that it would work out for the best?'

'I did not doubt you,' she assured him. 'All the same, it is a relief that it is over and that you were able to handle it so efficiently.'

He gave a modest bow at her compliment. 'I have dealt with worse, you know.'

'But I have never been forced to stand by, helpless, and watch you do it,' she said.

'And I knew from the first that your brother was no real threat.'

'Not a threat?' She stared at him in surprise. 'He is a liar and a cheat. I am his own sister and I have no idea what he might be capable of if backed into a corner.'

'As I said before, I have seen worse.' He gave her a pitying look. 'I am sorry to say it, my dear, but your brother is a coward. While he may think himself a dangerous man willing to do anything to save his own skin, he has never killed anything more ferocious than a doe. He attempted to trick me, just as you said he would. But his attempts were obvious and easy to predict. And half-hearted, as well.'

'I suppose you'd have done better,' she said, surprised.

'If I'd wanted my opponent dead?' Gerry thought for only a moment. 'I'd have dispensed with the nonsense and shot him point-blank before the duel started. Then I'd have sworn my second to secrecy and we'd have come back to the house with the corpse. Or I might have arranged a hunting accident. It would not have been as satisfying as seeing his face as I shot him, but it would have done the job.'

'Cold-blooded murder?'

Her husband shrugged. 'It is fortunate for all of us that I am an honourable man. But I also know what it truly means to fight for one's life. I have equal skill at killing men with sword or pistol. On several unfortunate occasions I used my bare hands. The people who speak of cold-blooded action as the greatest sin do not know what awful things can happen in the heat of the moment.'

For the first time since he'd been home, she saw the signs of tiredness and strain on his face. She had not expected him to be the young man who had left her. But he had aged a lifetime in seven years. 'There will be no more of either, once we have the house to ourselves.'

'My wife will paint me landscapes of Waterloo and I shall not slaughter so much as a rabbit ever again.' He sighed. 'It will be paradise, my dear.'

'For me, as well.' For a moment, she imagined

the quiet evenings and the freedom of unlocked doors. Then an image of Stewart playing on the hearth rug in the sitting room flitted across her mind. There had to be some way to persuade her husband to relent on his plans to send the boy away. But that discussion could wait until bedtime, when he was in the most receptive mood possible.

Gerry sighed, contented. 'I am well pleased that today went as it did. I settled your brother with a minimum of bloodshed. Your father and I have come to an understanding without the need for firearms.'

'And the guests have all run back to London,' she said with a smile.

'All but Greywall,' he reminded her.

'The earl?' For a moment, she had actually managed to forget him. Then the memory of the previous day rushed back. With it came the beginnings of a headache.

'He was bothering you yesterday,' Gerry said, matter-of-fact. 'And the boy,' he added.

'He suspects,' she said. It was a massive understatement of the situation. But it was all the explanation she meant to give. 'Thank you for acknowledging Stewart.'

'I'd have said anything to put the fellow off you,' Gerry said hurriedly, as if he wished to crush any hope she might have that he was softening. 'And what goes on in this house is no business of his, no matter how often he tries to make it so.'

Her chest tightened, imagining what he might have said. 'Has he been making trouble?'

Gerry nodded. 'Since long before you arrived here. He was lurking about the property even before Father died, hoping that our diminished fortunes would be a reason to sell. When Father refused, he tried to hunt our land without permission and had to be escorted to the property line like a common poacher.' Gerry shook his head. 'The man is repellent. I will take great pleasure from sending him away again as soon as I am able.'

Not now. At this prolonged talk of Greywall, she could feel the beginning of another attack. This time she fought against it, focusing on the memory of her husband's hands on her face and body and his own steady breathing. When she was sure she was calm enough to speak, she said, 'I do not think it is wise to antagonise him. He may be an old drunkard, but he is still a very powerful man.'

'Do not worry. I will handle the matter as discreetly as possible.' But as he said it, he smirked, as if the prospect of doing just the opposite were actually the plan.

An altercation between the two of them would be a disaster. It was not just a matter of the secrets that would be revealed, it was Gerry's likely response to them. They were so close to having the peaceful future that they wanted. She did not want to dredge up the past again and she certainly could not stand another duel.

'Let me,' she said suddenly.

'Let you what?' he asked, surprised.

'I would like to be the one to send the earl away.' He looked doubtful, so she said, 'You have promised me often enough that I can have anything I want. After seven years of his company, I would like to tell him what I think of him and send him home.'

'Won't the conflict with a guest be upsetting to you?' he said, frowning. 'I will not be responsible for causing a megrim by letting you deal with something that should be my responsibility.'

She forced a laugh, even as she felt the growing cluster of pain behind her eyes. 'Do not worry yourself that the man who could not even watch the morning's duel without fainting will cause an upset in me. He is old and harmless and I am quite capable of sending him packing.' As long as her son stayed in the nursery, well out of the way.

Gerry was still staring at her, as if he could not quite understand what he was hearing. But at last he said, 'Very well. If that is what you want, I see no real harm in sharing the fun of turfing out the guests. But if he gives you any trouble...'

'I will get you immediately,' she said, forcing a smile and kissing him on the cheek.

They parted when they arrived at the house. Lily went to her bedroom, Gerry presumed. But he went immediately to the back of the house to find Mrs Fitz. He did not bother to ring, but went down the stairs to the kitchen dining room, where he found both her and Aston, taking their coffee before beginning their day.

They looked up at him in surprise and answered in unison, 'Captain?' before preparing to stand.

He held up a hand, indicating that they remain seated. 'Just a question and then you may return to your breakfasts. Does the household keep lists of the guests that have been here?'

Mrs Fitz nodded. 'It is easier to keep track of the preferences of repeat visitors if some record is kept.' She frowned. 'There have not been many of those. But still.'

'Very sensible of you.' He gave her an approving smile. 'And how far back might those lists go? All the way back to the time I left?' He raised an encouraging eyebrow.

'I should think so, sir.' The woman frowned. 'I would have to go through my old diaries. But they are in the still room.' She rose again, ready to get them.

He waved her back to her seat. 'The matter is not urgent.' It had waited seven years. Another day would not matter. 'Later, when you are not too busy, could you compile me a list, complete with the names of any servants?'

'Of course, Captain.'

He thought for a moment. 'And include the bedrooms they occupied.'

She looked flustered. 'Is some item missing? Because then you would be right to include the servants. I doubt that any of the guests...' She stopped, perhaps remembering the character of the people that the Norths entertained.

'No,' he insisted. 'Nothing missing.' Not exactly. 'I just wish to know the details of what has been going on in the house in my absence.'

One detail in particular.

Mrs Fitz nodded obediently. 'Of course, sir. I will see to it today and you shall have the completed list by breakfast tomorrow.'

'Very good.' By then, the rest of the guests would be packing and he would have as much time as he needed to ferret out the one thing on which his wife had been curiously reticent. If she had lied, he would find out the reason for it. There would be no punishment for it, of course. She had suffered enough.

There was but one who truly deserved to pay for the incident. And if that man still took breath, he would not be doing so for long.

Chapter Eighteen

After returning from the duel, Lily spent more than her usual amount of time on her toilette before seeking out the earl. Perhaps if she waited long enough, something might occur that would make this meeting unnecessary.

Of course, she had been waiting and hoping for years already. So far, no miracle had come to dislodge the man from her house. If she waited any longer, Gerry would handle it himself, just as he had the rest of the guests. It was a potential disaster that could not be allowed.

Her maid had chosen a white-muslin day gown with a faint red stripe. After considering for a moment, Lily chose a red spencer that closed with a row of gold frogs. She had bought it specifically because it reminded her of her husband's uniform. She smiled at her reflection in the cheval glass. If one was to meet the enemy on the battlefield, then it did not hurt to be smartly attired. Though it seemed excessive for daytime, she let the maid decorate her dressed hair with a single coq feather that reminded her of the plume on a helmet. Then she left her room and went to the main floor to seek out her nemesis.

The house already had the too-quiet, empty feel that it got when the guests were gone. Without half a dozen noisy idiots in residence to distract her, the sound of her slippers echoing on the parquetry was unnerving. But the sort of person who was frightened of the sound of her own footsteps would never survive her talk with Greywall.

She stopped dead in the hall, listening to the sound of her own breathing to be sure it was steady and slow. Then she changed her pace, skipping like a child for a few steps and enjoying the syncopated reverberations it created. She was Lillian Wiscombe, wife of the hero of Salamanca. This was her house. She could walk, skip or even run through the halls if she wished to.

And she did not have to put up with unwanted guests.

She found the earl in the trophy room, staring up at the mounted head of a stag as if he coveted it. When he looked down at her, his face held the same expression.

'Lord Greywall,' she said.

'Lillian,' he said with a wolfish smile.

'I did not give you permission to use my name,' she said, trying to ignore the nervous hitch in her pulse when she looked at him.

'Surely, after all these years, there is no reason for us to be formal.'

'On the contrary,' she said. 'I thought I've made it clear that I have no desire to talk to you at all, much less to be informal.'

He smiled sadly. 'That is a shame. Now that the house is nearly empty, I hoped there would be reason to know you better.' It would be impossible to call the look he was giving her anything but a leer.

'I already know you better than I care to,' she said. 'And the house will be even emptier soon. My husband wants you to leave.'

'He has not said so,' the earl said, feigning in-nocence.

'Because I requested that he allow me to speak to you. I wish you gone, as well.'

He clutched at his heart as though her words wounded him. 'You would send me away after all we have meant to each other?'

'You mean nothing to me,' she said, feeling her throat tightening again. She swallowed and waited for it to relax.

'But you are one of my fondest memories,' he said. 'The night we spent together, during that first house party...'

The air seemed to rush out of the room and her head filled with the buzzing that preceded the worst of her megrims. 'You remember.'

'Of course. Have I ever said that I'd forgot-ten it?'

He had not. He had not mentioned it until those hints the other day. But then, in all these years, she'd taken great care to never be alone with him. 'I thought, perhaps, you were so inebriated that you did not realise what you had done. But if you remember it so well, the least you could do is apologise for it.'

'What about that night do I have to be sorry for?' he said, seeming honestly surprised. 'It was a pleasant interlude. I am surprised that we did not repeat it. Your husband was away for a long time. You must have been very lonely.'

'A pleasant interlude?' For the first time when facing him, her anger banished the fear. 'Perhaps you enjoyed it. But I remember being assaulted by a stinking drunk.' She was not shouting, but it felt as if she were. Her voice had no trace of the ridiculous breathiness it got when she was forced to speak to him. And her head was almost clear.

'If it was so awful, then why didn't you complain to someone?' He gave her an annoyingly triumphant smile.

'You should consider yourself fortunate that I haven't,' she said. 'It would not have gone well for you if I'd come forward with the truth.'

'Gone well for me?' At this, the earl laughed. 'My dear lady, when one reaches a certain rank it is exceptionally difficult for things to go any way but well. You would accuse me, I would call you a lying whore and that would be that.'

It was exactly the threat she had expected

seven years ago, when she had decided to stay silent.

'It will be even worse if you intend to defame me now,' he said.

'In what way?'

'Now that the good captain has exposed your father and brother for the cheats they are, they cannot afford to have me go to the law.'

'Is that what you think?' she said, taking measured breaths as she waited for him to finish.

'If you accuse me, I will tell everyone that you are from a family of criminals and that you were nothing more than a part of the entertainment.'

'An entertainer.' His threats were foul. But they were nothing but words. *Inhale. Exhale. Inhale.*

'I paid well for the use of you, my dear. Your family has done irreparable damage to my fortunes over the years. It will take more than one night to equal the money they took.'

'What is between my father, my brother and you is none of my affair,' she said. 'My husband and I want no part of it.'

'And what about the boy?'

'What of him?' Her bravery was a sham. She

could feel the blood rushing from her head, as her vision narrowed to a tunnel.

'He is mine, of course.'

'He is *mine*,' she said, and felt her strength returning. Stewart was hers and she would fight for him. 'He is mine. And the captain's,' she added. 'He told you so.'

'He might not know the truth, my dear. But we do.'

She ignored the tremor of unease that went through her, taking care to keep her voice calm. 'I was not sure what you knew. You have said nothing about that, either.'

'I had no desire to. It is not as if I wanted to acknowledge him. I was quite happy with things as they were.'

'I suppose you were,' she agreed. Perhaps if he had been a less repellent specimen, she might have demanded he pay to educate the child he had fathered, instead of hiding the boy from him.

'But if you have suddenly decided to put me out, you are forcing my hand. I suggest you take a more cooperative attitude in regard to my stay here and my attentions to you. If you do not, I will go to the law and tell my tale. Your father and brother will go to gaol, where they belong. And then I will go to Wiscombe and tell him the truth about his son.' He was sneering at her as if he expected immediate capitulation.

Something inside of her snapped. The last of the headache was gone, burst like a bubble, leaving a dangerous clarity behind. 'Those are your plans, are they?'

He gave a nod.

'Then let me answer your threats. Do what you will to my father and brother. If they do not have the skill to evade the law, they are no longer worthy of the North name. And as for Stewart? I made Gerald aware of the issues with his parentage the day of his return.'

'You told him?' By the shocked look on his face, the earl had obviously not expected this response. 'Why?'

She smiled. 'Because I tell my husband everything. Almost everything, that is. I told him that my attacker was dead because I feared what might happen if he learned that you still resided under his roof.' Her smile widened. 'He threatened violence. But there are only so many duels he can fight in a single week. Though he did handle the one this morning with no real effort. I had not expected there would be so much blood…'

The earl went pale. Although he did not mind the blood of animals, humans were another matter entirely. He rallied. 'He would not dare touch me. I am a peer.'

'He is very protective of me,' she said. 'And Stewart, as well.' That was nothing more than wishful thinking, but she said it anyway before returning to the truth. 'Just this morning, he was telling me of his exploits in the war. Did you know he is capable of killing a man with his hands?'

'But that was a Frenchman,' the earl said, his voice quavering.

'He shot my brother over a card game,' she explained. 'And he was barely annoyed about that. Can you imagine what he might be like if his anger was aroused?'

'Ronald North deserved worse than he got,' Greywall insisted.

'Just as you do. I begged him to be merciful to my brother, but I have no such soft feelings for you. One word from me and there will be no safe place in England for you.'

'He would hang for attacking an earl,' Greywall said.

'If he got caught, he would,' she agreed. 'But if you threaten me or my son, I doubt he would care. I suspect he would act first and face the consequences after. That is why I kept your secret. I do not want to see my husband risk arrest for avenging my attack. But if he finds out what you did, I doubt I would be able to stop him.'

'You would not dare tell him,' he said. But he didn't sound as sure as he had.

'And neither should you. You have nothing to hold over me, my lord. If you tell your secret, he will end you.' Her smile turned into a grin. 'Do not think you can leverage me into becoming your mistress or make me abide your odious presence for one day longer. My husband will be putting you out of the house tomorrow and I have no intention of coming within ten yards of you ever again. If you do not like it, go ahead. Do your worst. It will not matter which of us reveals the truth, you will be the one to face the consequences.'

Chapter Nineteen

The breakfast table was almost empty. Gerry smiled into his coffee, imagining how much better it would be when the last three guests were gone. As soon as they were, he would insist that Mrs Wiscombe move down the table to sit at his side instead of languishing at the far end. With her little red coat and a feather tucked behind one ear, she made such a fetching little soldier that when she joined them, he'd offered her a salute.

She'd responded with a cool smile of her own and a slight nod to tell him that her mission had been successfully accomplished.

There was a rattle of cutlery and a low curse as Ronald North struggled to cut his kipper with his left hand. Even with an improved bandaging and a few stiff drinks before breakfast, he was obviously in a great deal of pain.

Gerry ignored the grumbling and smiled left and right to the North gentlemen on either side of him. 'Well, my friends, now that the party is ending, have you given any thought to your future plans?'

'I plan to find some food that I can actually eat,' Ronald said, throwing his knife aside.

'It is fortunate that drinking only takes a single hand,' Gerry said, still smiling. 'You can do that anywhere. But your other favourite activities will be lacking here, now that we have no plans to entertain. Amongst the family, there is little point in playing cards for anything dearer than buttons. I am declaring a moratorium on billiards until I can procure a new table. And there will be no more hunting.'

'No hunting?' The elder North looked shocked at the idea. 'But Wiscombe Chase is a hunting lodge.'

'Perhaps the next generation will wish to take up a weapon and stalk game, but I have no interest in it,' Gerry replied.

'Does Stewart like to hunt, Lillian?' Ronald

pushed his plate aside and stared down the table at his sister.

Confronted with the last hurdle to their happiness, his wife flushed as scarlet as her coat and did not answer. But neither did she appear to be suffering from shortness of breath or headache that such an attack would have caused only a few days before.

No matter what Ronald was up to, Gerry refused to be drawn into a discussion at the breakfast table that might upset her newfound equilibrium. 'That matter can be established at a later time.'

She shot him a smile and a look of such hope that he prayed she had not misinterpreted the statement as anything other than an effort to silence her brother. It was immaterial to him whether Stewart hunted or not. Whichever choice he made, it would not be exercised on Wiscombe lands.

'But no hunting,' North said, still amazed. 'Surely an exception will be made for your neighbour, the earl.'

What the devil was North attempting now?

There was no way that the earl would be allowed to return once he'd been evicted from the house.

'Yes, indeed, Captain,' the earl said. 'Your wife has explained to me your desire for privacy. Though you wish the house to yourself, you cannot mean to close the grounds to me, as well. I have been hunting them so long, I feel as if they are my own.' There was no humility in the smile that accompanied this outrageous request. Only the annoying assumption that, since his ancestors had been given a title, he should be allowed to be where he was not welcome.

As she usually was at the table, Lily remained silent. But her eyes smouldered with irritation at the suggestion that the earl might still be wandering the land.

Gerry offered him a sympathetic shrug. 'Alas, my lord, I mean to stand firm on this. No hunting. None by anyone.'

'Well, we are not gone yet,' North said with a smile. 'We will pack tonight and be gone tomorrow. But there is still time to hunt today.'

The earl brightened. 'One last hunt, Wiscombe. And then I will leave you. Now that the cits are not here scaring the game with their common behaviour, I might finally get a shot at that champion stag of yours.'

'I am sure that the London accents were the only things standing between you and old Rex,' Gerry said, not bothering with an idiot's grin to put the man at ease.

North ignored his sarcasm. 'An intimate hunt. It is such a wonderful idea that I am amazed we have not done it before. I will accompany you, Lord Greywall.' Now North was the one grinning. As usual, his was harmless, affable and extremely persuasive. 'It is ages since I have been out in the fresh air.'

'You are so rarely out in the woods—you have no idea what trails the stag might use,' Ronald said, irritably.

'Then we shall take Wiscombe with us,' North said, with one of his most convincing smiles. 'He will be an even better guide than you because it is his land. He must know it better than any man in England.' His smile dimmed. 'At least, I should hope so.' He gave Gerry a doubtful look. 'But if it has been too long, or if you and your horse are not in fit condition for a few jumps...'

Was the man actually challenging him to prove

his worth as horseman? Gerry was pushing back from the table automatically before his brain reminded him that, with his father-in-law, nothing was so clear-cut that it could be understood on first hearing. Had Ronald's comment really been a sign of his contrary nature, of a part of some carefully prepared script?

'I suppose I could accompany you,' Gerry said, slowly, looking from one face to the next, trying to find the trap.

'I thought you said you did not enjoy hunting.' Greywall was equally suspicious.

Gerry shrugged. 'Not usually. But Ronald is in no condition to go, with only one hand to hold the gun.'

At this, Ronald glared up the table at him like the petulant child he was.

'And Lord Greywall should not be forced to take to the woods alone if he is truly interested in sport,' North said. 'He would not be able to drag such a huge stag alone.'

'Surely a footman or two could be spared,' Gerry said, looking at him even more suspiciously. Perhaps after seeing what had happened to his son, North wished to get him into the woods and put a bullet in his back, on purpose, by mistake.

If so, he would be disappointed. Once they were clear of the house, and of Lily, North and Greywall could attack. He would defend himself to the death, if necessary. At least the matter would be settled today. He refused to spend his life looking over his shoulder, waiting to be shot.

'Footmen were good enough for those London commoners. But surely, since it is Lord Greywall, you should be our guide,' North insisted.

'Oh, ho. I had forgotten that this was for the benefit of Lord Greywall,' Gerry said, unable to contain his sarcasm. 'Of course, you are right. A peer cannot be sent out in the company of servants.'

'If you do not wish to take me today, perhaps another time...' The earl was deliberately forgetting that there would be no more visits.

'Since this will be your last hunt here, I wish you all the luck you deserve.'

Lily had spoken. It was such an odd occurrence at the table that all the men looked up in surprise.

'As my husband said, we are having no more

hunting parties.' Her eyes were as wide and innocent as a true North. But there was no accompanying smile. 'I am sorry, my lord. Despite your desire to return as a valued neighbour, you will not be roaming our land like a stray dog. Once you leave Wiscombe Chase tomorrow, you will not be coming back. And today, my husband will accompany you to make sure you know the boundaries of the property so there will be no accidental incursion.'

'But what if I cannot manage to take the stag?' The earl was still trying to gain a reprieve.

'You have been trying for years,' Lily reminded him. 'I think it is time to admit that the poor animal has beaten you.'

'I will never admit that,' the earl said, glaring at her so venomously that Gerry felt the hairs on his neck rising in protective anger.

'Then I am sorry you cannot accept the fact that there are some things on this property that you just...can't...have.' The expression on her face as she stared back at him was totally unfamiliar. Gerry had never seen her approach conflict with anything more than panic and pain. But this morning she was clear-headed and angry. The look in her eyes said, no matter what others in the room might say, she would not be moved.

'We will discuss it when I return,' the earl said. 'Perhaps a payment…'

'There will be no discussion. The discussion is over. I am decided. No amount of money will change my mind.'

Was it his influence that had changed her so? He'd have liked to have taken the credit, but he doubted it. Perhaps he had sparked something in her. But whatever burned now was too bright to be attributed to his doing. He offered an encouraging smile and another subservient salute, but she did not even look in his direction. It left him feeling as if he'd caught something far beyond his power to hold.

This new strength was all her. And it was magnificent. She was holding the earl's gaze with no sign of submission. In the end, he was the one to look away. 'Captain Wiscombe, can you not control your wife?'

'Apparently not, my lord,' Gerry answered.

'Then I will have to take the stag today.' He pointed to North and Gerry. 'The two of you will help me. Tonight the haunch will be served at dinner, and the head and horns will go back with me to Greywall tomorrow.'

If that is what will get you to leave, thought Gerry. They would be chasing after the impossible. Rex, as he always had, would slip away into the moors, hiding where no man could follow. Orion himself could not trap the beast. Then he smiled and said aloud, 'Of course. I have been tracking old Rex since I was a boy and know all his favourite places. Unless he has changed his direction, I will lead you right to him.' But Greywall be damned, he would make sure that it was done from the windward side so Rex caught their scent and left nothing but tracks in the mud.

'The sooner we start the better.' The earl pushed his plate aside and rose from the table. 'Have the servants load the weapons and we will go.' Then he was gone to check his guns and saddle his horse.

Gerry lingered at the table a moment longer, since his wife remained at her place, smiling and sipping her chocolate. She looked up at him, her huge dark eyes shaded by long lashes. 'Do you wish a kiss for luck in today's hunt?' The words were weighted with strange and dangerous emotions, and he was thankful that none of them seemed to be directed at him.

'If you wish to give me one,' he said, cautiously.

She stood and put her arms around him, delivering a kiss that left him dazed. Several days had given his sweet and innocent wife a surprising amount of skill. Then she released him, staring up with a strange half-smile. 'Good luck to you, my captain. Share none of it with the earl. And if you care for me at all, do not let him shoot that stag.'

'I had no idea that you cared about the poor beast,' he said, in surprise.

'My only wish it that Greywall returns to his home empty handed and unsatisfied. Do that for me and I will be the most grateful of wives.' She batted her lashes again.

'Very well, my lady.' He smiled back at her.

Chapter Twenty

'I have never gone so far from the house, when hunting with Ronald,' the earl said, glancing around him at the thinning trees. Gerry had led their little party nearly three miles already, until they approached the tor that marked the little strip of moor at the back of the property.

'That might explain your lack of success,' Gerry said, urging Satan up a narrow path through the rocks. 'If Rex has been hiding from you, this is the place he would choose.' He offered up a silent apology to the beast for sharing that knowledge at all.

Though he had no intention of disappointing Lily, the challenge of hunting without finding anything was more difficult than he'd thought.

Especially since Rex seemed as interested in stalking them as the earl was in shooting him.

The stag was keeping pace with them, walking silently at their flank and awarding Gerry an occasional glimpse of hoof or tail before disappearing into the trees again. Gerry pretended to ignore him and made no move to alert the other hunters. Eventually, Rex would bore with the game and go back to his home on the moor. Since Greywall was either too drunk or too foolish to notice what was not directly in front of him, he would likely never realise how close he came to success.

'I told you that the presence of the captain would make a difference,' North called from the rear. 'Magnificent country,' he added, directing this to Gerry.

Gerry grunted in return. As far as he could tell, it was magnificently useless. Beautiful, of course. But not the sort of place they wanted to be caught in after dark. Without a clear view of the terrain and a stout stick to test the ground, the risk of ending up knee deep in a bog far outweighed the pleasure of a moonlit walk.

'Is this still your property?' They were as far

away from the Greywall lands as it was possible to be. It was plain that, without a guide, the earl might never find his way home.

And what a tempting idea that was. But not necessary. One more day and the man would be gone for good, even if Gerry had to pack the bags and carry them himself. 'Do you doubt my knowledge of the property lines?'

At this, the earl laughed and Gerry could hear the rattling and sloshing of the flask as the man took a drink. 'You sound very like your father. He had an obsession with borders and boundaries, as I remember.'

It was not a reminder he welcomed. Today, his father was already uncomfortably close. Gerry had had no desire to soil his new hacking jacket, so he'd had Mrs Fitz hunt up some leather breeches and an old poacher's coat. Both still stank of the old man's tobacco. 'You should be grateful that I know the land as well as he did.' He reined in his horse and held a hand up to call for silence. Then he pointed towards the last stand of trees before the moor. There was a flash of russet, just out of rifle range before Rex disappeared deeper into the wood.

'I'll be damned,' said the earl, fumbling for his gun.

'Quite possibly,' North agreed. 'But you might have your stag before then.'

The voice behind him raised the hairs on the back of Gerry's neck. If North was an enemy, he had made the worst mistake of his life by allowing the man to follow him. Best to change the order of things. Gerry dismounted. 'From here, we go on foot. Keep your gun at the ready, Greywall. I will circle and try to flush him towards you.'

He made a wide circuit of the trees, going halfway up into the granite boulders before stopping to check the wind. From here, the breeze would carry his scent straight to the stag. That alone would be enough to urge a younger and less intelligent animal towards North and the earl. But Rex would know better. He had been both smart and lucky enough to outlast Gerry's father. It was hard to believe that, even with help, the earl could succeed in taking him.

Or perhaps Rex's reign had finally come to an end. Gerry had not even reached the back of the copse before he heard the crack of a rifle and the triumphant shout of the earl. He turned and picked his way back to where he'd left his two companions.

'I hit him,' the earl exclaimed when he came into sight. 'And on the first shot. He is mine for sure.'

'An excellent shot,' North announced. 'The animal broke cover and, even uphill and into the sun, Greywall got him.'

Gerry glanced around him, relieved when he could not find so much as a drop of blood to indicate the bullet had found its target. 'Then where is the body?'

'It was not a clean death,' the earl said. 'But a killing shot, certainly. Let us run him down.' He turned to get back on his horse.

'Which direction did he turn?'

The earl pointed towards the moor.

Gerry held up a hand to stay him. 'The ground on the moor is too unstable to take the horses. One will turn an ankle for certain and we will be walking back.'

'Then we must track the deer on foot,' the earl announced, dismounting unsteadily and heading towards the bog.

The last thing Gerry wanted was to lead a drunkard on a jaunt across unstable ground. 'It is dangerous to stray too far from the forest, if you do not know the territory,' he said.

'There is nothing to fear,' the earl announced. 'We will only go as far as the body of the stag.

'He got off a good shot,' North agreed, then added to the earl, 'The poor fellow will be bleeding. He will not make it far and will leave a clear trail for you to follow.'

'All the same, it is better to be prepared.' Gerry turned back to his saddle to get his stick, a knife and a stout length of rope. They would be necessary in the event that he needed to drag the animal back. But more likely, the slight delay in equipping himself would give the quarry a fighting chance to run for his life.

'You are taking too long,' the earl opined. 'We must get to him while there is still light.'

'If the shot was as good as you say, we do not need to rush.'

'You selfish bastard. My last hunt and you expect me to be frightened of a bit of wet grass. I will go ahead. Follow when you are ready.'

'That is most unwise, my lord.' There were

a hundred things he might have said about the differing weight of man and deer, and the superior knowledge that even a frightened animal had of the dangerous terrain of the moor. The whole area was full of featherbeds and shifters. Patches of moss or gorse that looked solid might drag an unsuspecting hunter to a watery death. But he barely had time for the brief phrase he'd shouted at Greywall's retreating back. The earl was so eager for his stag that he was already up the tor and disappearing over it.

'Be careful,' North called cheerfully, getting down off his horse. 'I am certain the earl will take care,' North said, to reassure him.

'He is just as likely to get himself killed,' Gerry replied, cursing quietly as he dug in his saddle bag.

'We all must go some time.' The words were accompanied by the chick of a cocked pistol. 'May I see your empty hands, Captain Wiscombe?'

Gerry cursed himself for being distracted and for not bringing the pistol that would have been in this very bag had he been in Portugal and not his own back garden. He turned to display his empty hands to his father-in-law.

'Very good.' North was as cheerful as ever. He gestured with the gun. 'Could you step away from your rifle as well? Take a seat on that rock.'

'Do you mean to shoot me sitting down?' Gerry asked. 'It would be just as easy to do it standing.'

'Shoot you?' for a moment, North seemed puzzled. 'I merely wish a few moments of uninterrupted conversation.'

'You can get that just as easily without pointing a pistol at me,' Gerry suggested, then walked slowly towards the indicated seat. In his mind, he calculated the steps to his gun and the cover of the woods. He did not want to shoot both of his wife's family in the same day. But neither did he want to die with a ball in him, when success was so close.

From the moor, there was an echoing cry for help.

Without thinking, Gerry turned and took a step in the direction of the tor.

'Stop!'

He froze again, remembering the gun. 'The

earl is hurt. We must go to him. You have my word that we will settle what is between us once he is safely off the moor.'

'Sit down, Wiscombe. There is nothing between us that needs settling,' North said, still smiling. 'The only problem I have with you is your predictable desire for heroic action.'

'Some of the bogs are deep,' Gerry reminded him. 'This is not one of your little games that hurts no one. He may be drowning.' When North made no move to put away the pistol, he added, 'We must help him before it is too late.'

To add weight to his logic, there was another call for help, followed by a man's scream of terror.

Instead of being moved to action, North leaned against the nearest tree. 'If we are lucky, it is too late already.'

'Damn it, man. Let me go to him.' He did not like the earl, but neither did he want to drag the man's body back from what should have been his final hunt.

'A little while longer, I think,' North said. 'I feared we would have to wait through the night to do this properly. But things are progressing nicely.'

'I should never have let him go ahead.'

'And he should never have raped my daughter,' North said, with no change in his demeanour.

'He…' Now that the truth was before him, it made perfect sense. Lily's silence at dinner and the headaches after the meal. She'd been trying to be a perfect hostess while sharing a table with her attacker. 'She said he was dead.'

'She lied,' North said. 'I suspect she was worried about what would happen if you learned the truth. One cannot just shoot a peer, Captain Wiscombe.'

But he would have done it. He would not have been able to help himself. 'She should not be the one trying to protect me,' Gerry said, his guilt returning.

'But she is trying, all the same. She does not want to risk losing you,' North said. 'She loves you.'

'She loves the hero of Salamanca,' Gerry corrected.

'She deserves a hero,' her father agreed. 'She's seen damn few of them in her life. The North men have been chronic disappointments. As her father...' He shook his head. 'If I'd only known, the matter would have been settled long before you got here. But I swear to God, I thought the child was yours. And that our estrangement...' And now, his voice broke. 'I gave the earl the master bedroom. I thought to flatter him. All this time she has been thinking I was a pandering villain and not just a trusting fool.'

'I told her that it could not have been intentional,' Gerry said.

North nodded. 'I am nowhere near the perfect father, but I would never allow anyone to hurt her. Since that has already happened, something needed to be done.'

'And the gun?' Gerry pointed at the pistol the man still held.

'There was going to be a hunting accident of some sort,' North said. 'But a habitual inebriate drowning in a bog will be much easier to explain at an inquest than a bullet in the back. If need be, you can swear that you were held at gunpoint and prevented from aiding the man until it was too late. In the eyes of the law, you are an innocent victim.'

'And the earl?' There had been no sound from the moors since that last unearthly scream.

'He got what he deserved,' North said, putting the gun aside. 'Time will tell if the Lord blesses you with a daughter, Wiscombe. If he does, you will find there are no limits to what you would do to keep her safe. And if you fail?' He shook his head. 'For your sake, I hope you do not.'

'But we cannot just let him drown,' Gerry said, knowing that they most certainly could. Hadn't he just told his wife that a convenient hunting accident would be easy to arrange?

'You've already made an effort to keep him from harm.' North's smile had returned. 'I distinctly heard you tell him that it was dangerous. Yet he went on ahead because he wanted that damned deer.'

That was true enough.

'It is a shame I could not be there to watch him suffer,' North said, with a sigh. 'But as my daughter pointed out at breakfast, we cannot always have what we want. I think it has been long enough now. Let us go and see what we can find of him.'

Gerry put the supplies he'd collected back in

the saddle bag and led the way, walking a skittish Satan over the tor and out on to the moor itself. There they found the blood trail from the stag, just as the earl had expected. But the red drops were sparse and the tracks gave no indication that the stag was weak on his feet. The even hoofprints were mirrored by the boot prints of a man.

They followed the marks barely a quarter mile before they discovered the earl. The clear trail ended suddenly, devolving into a muddy mess of hoofmarks and the claw-like troughs of a man's hands searching for purchase. Gerry tapped at the ground in front of him and found the place where it gave way to bog, watching the carpet of moss that covered the muck sway and ripple as he poked at it.

Then he took out his rope and tied one end of it to the saddle before slowly lowering himself into the hidden water. A few minutes searching beneath the surface and he was able to grasp a coat sleeve and tie the other end of the rope around the corpse. Then he climbed back on to the path and urged his horse back to drag the earl to the surface.

They stared down at the dead man.

'As I told you before, people who I invite here deserve what they get,' North said.

The late Earl of Greywall stared up at the sky with a blank look of surprise, his forehead marked by the bloody print of a single cloven hoof.

Chapter Twenty-One

It was taking too long.

Lily had never been interested in the hunts that were held almost daily at her home. But she could not help but be aware of the pattern they followed. Even the longest of them was over before dusk. It gave the participants time to wash, or more often to drink before dinner.

But tonight, the sun was almost fully set before she heard the sound of the men returning. She'd been waiting in the sitting room for some word of their progress and rushed towards the hall in time to hear the unusual request that a footman locate my lord's valet immediately.

'There has been an accident.'

The words sent a chill through her. It was

some comfort that her husband had been the one speaking.

And now her father said, 'He would not listen to reason. He was following that damn stag and he would not stop, even when the animal ran on to the moor.'

From the third member of the party, she heard nothing. If he were really hurt, she'd have expected swearing or complaints, or at least a demand for strong drink. The total silence was ominous.

She pushed her way through the knot of servants gathering in the doorway to see a body wrapped in oilcloth slung over the saddle of the earl's horse.

A hunting accident.

But Gerry did not know. He would have had no reason to take action against the earl.

At the moment, she could not enquire even if she wanted to. Gerry was in a quiet conversation with the white-faced valet, who was then stuffed into a coach to make the short ride to Greywall to get others who would come back to take the earl home. Until they arrived, Wiscombe servants were gathering to find a properly respectful place for the body of a peer.

Lily turned to Mrs Fitz to request a cold supper be laid for family and any servants of the earl that might be coming, and tried to decide if her current calm was an accurate reflection of her mood, or merely the shock that accompanied sudden death. In either case, it was more ladylike than joy.

She started forward, trying to get a better look at the body.

'Lillian.' Her father took her arm to lead her away.

'I need to know,' she whispered.

'He is dead. There is no question of that. Come away.' She tried to pretend that she had not seen the nod that passed between him and her husband that seemed to confirm her fears. 'Let us go back to the sitting room. There is nothing that can be done for him.'

She shut the sitting-room doors behind him, her calm disappearing. 'That is not what matters to me. I need to know which of you shot him.'

Her father let one inappropriate laugh escape

before he regained his own composure. 'What you mean to ask is, *What happened?*'

'Tell me,' she said, clutching his hand. 'Tell me that Gerald did not do something foolish on my account. Because I could not bear it.'

'The earl tracked a wounded stag on to the moors. We were not there to see his death. It appears the beast attacked him, either before or after he fell into a bog. The combination of the attack and the water...' Her father shook his head.

It really had been an accident. She sat, rather too quickly, on the sofa. But since the sudden bout of weakness was not followed by fainting, headaches or shortness of breath, it was likely a perfectly normal reaction.

'And what of the deer?'

'The deer?'

'Rex,' she said. 'The stag. I assume that was the animal he was chasing. What became of him?'

'A small wound. He's survived worse. Greywall was convinced that he was dying, of course. But circumstances proved him wrong.'

It was a relief. 'And you and Gerald.'

'Wet and tired. Nothing more.'

There was more to it than that, she was sure. It was all too perfectly convenient. Perhaps it would be best not to ask. But she could not help herself. 'When did you realise it was him?'

'When you told me, yesterday. There could be only one man you were speaking of.' He sat down beside her and took her hand. 'I did not know. If I had, there would have been a day like this one before Stewart was born.'

'It is better this way,' she said.

'But now that I have learned the truth? I hope the years of silence that have been between us is punishment enough.'

Even with the earl gone, there was still so much to forgive. 'Your little schemes were never easy for me,' she admitted. 'This problem with earl was simply the worst consequence of them.'

'I know, my dear.' He patted her hand.

'Are they finally over?'

'For you, at least,' he assured her. 'Ronald and I will be gone after supper. There are some markers that need to be cashed in before the rest of Greywall's creditors arrive.'

'And then, where will you go?'

He shrugged. 'I cannot tell. But we will not be returning here. We will send for our things when we are settled and tell you our direction.'

'You're leaving me?' For years, she had wished to be free of him and Ronald, and the life that they'd created for her. Now that it was here, she was not ready.

'I am sure, if you need me, I will not be difficult to find.' Then he smiled. 'But it may be easier for you if you do not look too hard.'

'You do not mean to change,' she said, sadly.

'Not in all things,' he said. 'I still believe that most people get what they deserve in life. But you did not deserve what happened to you and I am sorry for it. Now that your husband has come home to you, I will have no more worries about your happiness or safety. At least not as long as your brother and I keep our business clear of you.'

She leaned forward and kissed him on the cheek, still not sure how she felt. 'I think I will miss you,' she said.

'For that, I am glad.' He returned her kiss.

'And now, my dear, let us tend to the removal of the last thorn in your side. The earl is going home and will not return.'

Chapter Twenty-Two

It had not even been a week since her husband's return, but it felt as if an eternity of time had passed. She had not thought that a day would ever come where coming to her husband's room at night would be as natural as going to her own bed.

It would take some time to get used to the fact that her father and brother were gone. And possibly even more to assure herself that the earl would not reappear and refuse to leave without his trophy. But as long as she could have Gerry here, her love for him would ease the sting of partings and fears of the past.

'At last, we have the house to ourselves.' Gerry was grinning at her again, grey eyes sparkling and displaying those slightly uneven teeth that made him look like a mischievous little boy. But the way he patted the mattress at his side had nothing to do with innocence.

She thought of the reason that the house was empty and shivered. 'I am not sure it is entirely appropriate to feel happy after what has happened.'

'You are not actually mourning Greywall, after what he did to you.'

'How do you know...?' After she had taken such care that he not learn the truth.

'Your father explained the situation, while Greywall was having his accident. The man might be slow to realise some things, but once he is aware of the problem, he is quick to solve it.'

'While he was having an accident?' she repeated.

'He did not want my heroic instincts to overcome common sense and lead me to rescue Greywall before justice had been done.'

'Then it was not an accident,' she said.

'It was more of an accident than many things that have happened to people who cross the Norths,' he said. 'I doubt even your silver-tongued father can persuade a stag to attack on cue. The man also fell into the bog of his own accord. If I was slow to help?' He shrugged. 'It was because your father pulled a pistol on me and explained the need for circumspection.'

'He drowned the earl,' she said.

'Certainly not. He gave Greywall an opportunity. It is not his fault that the man was foolish enough to act on it.'

'You sound very like a North,' she said, unsure whether she liked the sensation of *déjà vu* the comment engendered.

'That was why we decided it was for the best that your father and brother leave as soon as possible. I will allow one such accident on my property since the man was deserving. But I do not mean for it to become a habit.'

'You wanted peace,' she said.

'And now I have it.'

'And no more death.'

He shrugged. 'Some things cannot be helped. It was quite possible that he was gone before I could have reached him. The man was drunk after breakfast and made no effort to see to his own safety. And Rex did not grow to be as old as he is without having tricks of his own. They may look gentle, but deer can be dangerous when wounded.'

'And I did want the stag to survive,' she said. She much preferred Rex to the earl.

'Despite it all, your father is not the scoundrel that your brother is,' Gerry said, and then added, 'I am sorry that I had to shoot him.'

'No, you're not,' Lily corrected.

He laughed in the firelight. 'You're right. I'm not. But I am glad that I did not have to shoot your father as well. Nor any of the guests. Not even the one who deserved it most.'

'Let us not speak of him again,' she said, leaning close to kiss him.

'Never,' he agreed. 'But with the lot of them gone, our house is almost back to normal.'

'Almost,' she said, suddenly remembering what was still let to settle.

'I must find a school for your son, of course. The one my father sent me to is a good distance away. But it is certainly rigorous enough to prepare him for Cambridge. I will write tomorrow to see if any of my old schoolmasters remain and if they would consider taking a first-year student in the middle of a term.'

He was droning on about the distant future. Those details were not the least bit important right now. 'He is a bit young to start, is he not…?' she began carefully. 'He is not quite seven.'

'He will adjust,' Gerry said, frowning.

'But will I?' She marshalled her fears and took a steadying breath. 'We have never been apart. And once he has started school, I will not see him for months at a time.'

'More than months,' he reminded her, oblivious to her pain. 'He will be spending his holidays there. If the school cannot house him, perhaps there are some farms in the area that have room for a boarder.'

'Farms?' she said, her voice turning shrill. 'Next you will have him working for his keep like a common labourer.',

'Certainly not,' he said, surprised at her reaction. 'He will be raised as a gentleman. You will be able to write him any time you like to assure yourself of his progress,' he added, as an afterthought.

'He is barely able to read a letter at his age,' she snapped.

'The schoolmasters will read to him. And the other boys.'

'No!' The word came out as a shout that surprised them both. Her plan had been to coax and cajole. She'd meant to use her feminine wiles, to be biddable and agreeable as she always was. But despite how much had changed since his return, it was clear that his plans for Stewart had not changed at all.

'In a year or so, it might be easier for him,' she said in a calmer voice.

'Perhaps it might.' He gave her a stern look. 'But we will have to make do with the plan as it is.'

She rolled closer to him, so their thighs touched, placing her hands flat against his chest so she might feel the beat of his heart. 'I had hoped, now that you know more about the circumstances of his birth, that you might reconsider the severity of your future plans.'

'They are not severe,' he replied, covering her hands with his in an effort to calm her. 'They are sensible. If we are ever to put the incident behind us, we cannot have the boy running about the house, always in sight and underfoot.'

'The incident?' she said in what she hoped was a warning tone. She had been calm too long and it had availed her nothing.

'It is not healthy for you to brood upon it,' he answered, with surprising gentleness. 'I have seen how it upsets you when you are reminded of it.'

'I do not brood upon it,' she insisted. 'In fact, I managed quite well, despite seeing my attacker almost every day at meals.'

'You had occasional spells,' he reminded her. 'And nightly headaches.

'Sometimes the fear did get the better of me,' she said, annoyed that he was right.

'You will be even better now that Greywall is gone. And once we have sent the boy away...'

'Stewart,' she said. 'His name is Stewart.' It was one thing to want justice and quite another to think that the past could be erased if one did not look at it.

'Once Stewart has gone to school,' he corrected, 'it will be even easier.' He squeezed her hands again and slipped his arms around her, ready to pull her close and end the discussion with a kiss.

She took another breath and said firmly, 'It will not.' Then she pushed away from him and sat up.

He reached for her, as surprised by her rejection as by her words.

'The spells and headaches are all but gone, now that you are here,' she said. 'Knowing that you understand and forgive me, and having support, was all I really needed to heal.' He must see that she had changed. Everything was different now. Only her love for Stewart was unchanged. 'I was able to stand up to the earl myself this morning, with no trouble at all. He'd have left as planned, even without your and Father's arranged accident.'

'That is good to know,' he said, obviously surprised. 'But even if he'd left, he would not really be gone. His son would remain.'

'Stewart is not his son,' she said. 'He is mine. To his dying breath, the earl did not know him, or claim him.'

'Perhaps not,' Gerry admitted. 'But that does not change how he came to be in my house.' The inflection was subtle, meant to remind her that while the house belonged to him, the child never would.

'But nothing that happened here was Stewart's fault. It is not fair to punish him for what his father did.'

'I am not punishing him,' Gerry insisted.

'Then you are punishing me,' she said. That was what this would be, whether he knew it or not.

'I am not punishing you. I am trying to spare you pain.' If he thought that was true, it showed how little he knew her.

'But he does not cause me any pain. There are nothing but sweet memories when I think of him.' She touched his arm, to assure him that she was fine.

'That makes no sense,' Gerry said.

'You cannot understand,' she said 'You are not a mother. Even though I hated his father, Stewart is as much a part of me as my own heart. To take him away would be like ripping that organ out of my chest.'

'You are right,' he said. 'I do not understand, because it does not make sense. To have him here would be a continual reminder to me of what happened.'

'A continual reminder to you,' she said and felt her own anger rising again. 'That is what this is really about. Your fine words about sparing me pain are nothing more than that. The truth is this: your pride is wounded. You do not want to think that, even unwilling, I was ever with another man.'

'I do not blame you,' he said quickly. 'I blame myself.'

'Do you not see?' She shook her head. 'Blaming anyone other than the earl is quite pointless. My father did not plan for it to happen. I could not have stopped it and neither could you. We were both little more than children when it occurred . And Stewart is the most innocent of all.'

'That may be true,' Gerry allowed. 'But you ask too much of me if you expect me to take him into my home and treat him as my own son.'

'And you ask too much of me, if you want me to give him up,' she said. A rush of fear came with the words. But for the first time in for ever, there was no light-headedness, or blinding pain. The truth terrified her, but it was a relief to face it. 'I want to make you happy and be the loyal wife you want. But I cannot do that at Stewart's expense.'

'But you are my wife.' Faced with her sudden insurrection, Gerry did not sound so much angry as bewildered.

'And I promised to obey you in all things,' she agreed. 'I have discovered that I cannot keep my promise to you.'

Now he was the one acting as if the wind had been knocked from his sails. It took some time before he was able to answer at all. 'What are we to do?'

It was the first time he had asked for her opinion. It might have pleased her had she an answer that would bring them both happiness.

'I do not see an answer, other than separation. I will go and take Stewart with me. It will spare you from having to be reminded of what happened,' she said, trying to keep the bitterness from her voice.

'I will not give you money to maintain your own household, if that's what you are after,' he said, showing a trace of the anger she had seen on the day he'd arrived.

'You will not need to,' she said. 'I have enough saved from the allowance you gave me that the two of us can live comfortably for quite some time.' If that failed, there was always her father. He was barely out of her life. Was it a sign of strength or weakness if she was to go back to him so soon?

'How very sensible of you to see to your own future,' he said in a dry tone. 'Now what am I to do with my mine, if I have a wife who refuses to live with me?'

'There might be a way to gain an annulment, even after all this time,' she said. 'If you can prove fraud.'

'There was nothing havey-cavey about it,' he said indignantly. 'The licence was legal and the banns were read.'

She sighed. 'My family specialises in making crooked things seem straight. How hard can it be to do the reverse? And a legal separation would net you nothing. It would not allow you to marry again.'

'Or you,' he reminded her.

'I have no intention of seeking another husband.' Even the thought of replacing Gerry made her heart ache.

He gave her a sardonic leer. 'Have I ruined you for all other men?'

'In a way,' she said. 'I love you. I expect I will continue to do so, even if we are apart. If I cannot be with you, then I will be happier alone.'

Apparently, she'd said a thing he could not joke his way out of, for he was silent again. Though it hurt that her declaration was not immediately followed by one from him, saying the words aloud had given her a freedom she'd never felt before. She loved him. He knew. If she had nothing else, she gained that.

But now, she must set him free. 'There is only one other alternative I can give you.'

'And what is that?' He was smiling as if he expected her to announce that she'd changed her mind and agreed with his initial plan, after all.

'If Stewart and I were to die, it would leave you free to marry and start again.'

'No.' The denial was quick and adamant.

'Not in truth. But it is far easier to arrange for two people to disappear permanently and appear dead than to navigate the courts to end a marriage.'

'You would have me live a lie, just so you could keep that child.' The bitterness in his voice as he said it proved to her that there would be no declaration of devotion forthcoming. His feelings for her were strong, but ultimately they were as selfish as her family's had been.

'When I give my heart, I do not ever take it back. It is true of my love for you,' she said, touching his cheek. 'But I love Stewart as well. Even if I could send him away, his existence will always be a barrier between us, whether you admit it or not.'

'Very well, then.' He rolled away from her. 'The sooner the better. You will leave in the morning and take the boy with you. Once you have found a place to settle, I will send your things on after you. And there will be no nonsense about faked deaths or rigged annulments. When you realise your mistake and come crawling back to me, we will settle things as I planned and that will be that.'

He stood for a moment, as if looking for a door to slam. And then he realised where they were and pointed at her. 'Remove yourself from my room, madam. You are no longer welcome here.'

'Yes, Captain,' she said and went back to her own room. The tears did not begin until she heard it lock behind her.

Chapter Twenty-Three

He was the last of the Wiscombes.

Gerry stared at the star-shot canopy of his bed and tried to accept the thing he had been trying to prevent. He'd got a wife and a fortune. He'd survived Waterloo to come home and father a child. He had spent a third of his life trying to stop the inevitable decay of house and name. And he had failed.

Now, Lily would take the child and go. Despite what he'd said about her seeing the error of her ways and returning to him, once she left his home he knew he would not get her back.

Eventually, he would give up on the past. There would be embarrassing legal ramblings as he tried to decide if it was even possible to dissolve this union. If the true parentage of the boy was revealed, it might be better off for him. Even the unacknowledged son of an earl might do quite well for himself, should Greywall's family be bullied into helping on the sly.

Lily would be utterly ruined by his efforts to be free. In the eyes of society, it would be better if she really died rather than feigning it. There would be no acceptance or forgiveness for her, even though nothing that had happened was her fault.

He would try to make it easy for her. Even if she did not wish or expect it, he would see that she lived comfortably and wanted for nothing. But if she left him, she would live and die alone. No honourable man would want a woman who had been cast off by her husband, even if it was at her own request. She was probably right that the best way to deal with things was a faked death and a new start for both of them.

Damn it all, he did not want another man to want her. She was his. She belonged at his side. When he'd left for the war, he'd been a foolish, infatuated child. When that had faded, he'd thought to hate her. But even as he tried, she'd haunted his dreams. If he'd lain with another, it was always while thinking of her. Would it hurt her, as she'd hurt him? Would her kisses be sweeter? Would her body be more lush? What would it be like when he finally returned home to her?

What was it like? It was like taking another sword in the side: red-hot burning agony. That wound had healed, but this one never would. He had found the perfect woman: loyal, loving, stalwart in adversity and beautiful inside and out. He'd held the other half of his own soul in his arms. After that, no other woman could ever satisfy him.

And now, just as he'd feared, she was leaving him for another man. What sweet irony it was that his rival was a waist-high toy soldier who hated horses. He was not wealthy or powerful. The circumstances of his birth did not matter. While she might claim to love Gerry with her whole heart, she would walk through fire for her son, sacrificing herself without a second thought.

He could not cast her off without destroying her. He could not replace her without destroying himself. Which meant there was no choice for him but do nothing at all to end the marriage and accept the fact that he was the last true Wiscombe.

Lily was standing over his bed, her hand clutching her key to the connecting door.

He felt a rush of foolish hope. She had reconsidered. She had found some solution he had not thought of that could satisfy her conscience and was returning to his bed. He held out his arms in welcome.

Then the hope faded. Her face ghostly pale in the moonlight. She was trembling. But not from cold, for she was fully dressed with a shawl about her shoulders.

He sat up, instantly alert. 'What is the matter?'

'Stewart,' she said in a tear-choked whisper. 'He is missing. Miss Fisher cannot find him anywhere. Nor can I. We searched the house from top to bottom. I looked in all his favourite hiding places.' Her trembling increased with the first shaking sobs.

'I am sure it is nothing,' he said. 'The boy is always wandering about. I have seen it myself.'

'In daylight, perhaps. But never at night.' She shook her head, trying to deny the obvious. 'He is outside. In the dark. You know the dangers of these woods. There are animals. Cliffs. Bogs.'

'He would not get as far as the moor without a horse,' he said. But that was hardly a reassurance to a worried mother.

She held out her hands in supplication. 'I know that you hate him...'

'Not hate, precisely,' he said, stunned at the unworthiness of his feelings towards a harmless little boy.

She ignored his denial and continued. 'Please, Captain Wiscombe, I have no one else to turn to.'

He swung his legs out of bed and pulled on his breeches, shrugging a coat over his nightshirt and tucking in the tails. 'You were right to come to me.' He was her husband. Who else would she go to in a time of desperate need? That she turned to him as a last resort pricked at his conscience. Even worse, he had become Captain Wiscombe again. Not her husband, but some near-fictional hero no more real than a news clipping.

If the hero of Salamanca was who she needed, that was who she would have. 'Wake the servants and have them search the house again. He may have slipped by you as you looked. I will search the grounds and you will see that it is nothing.' That was just as likely to be a lie as truth. He had grown up in this house and could name any number of things that a small child might wander into at night that were either dangerous or deadly.

But it did no good to alarm the child's mother, or to brood on them himself. He gave her an overly confident smile. 'I expect I will be back in an hour or less, hauling the little fellow by the ear.'

'Thank you.' Lily launched herself at him, pressing her body to his. 'Thank you, so.'

She was clinging to him as if he were hope and salvation and instinctively his arms went around her, to protect her. He had failed her once by leaving her alone and at risk. He had failed her again when he could not overcome his foolish pride and see that he had asked too much of her. He would not fail her twice in one night. But her present need did not entitle him to hold her now.

Carefully, he set her aside. 'I will take care of

everything. Wait for me here. I will be back in no time.'

She sat down on the edge of his bed, pressing herself back into the headboard and hugging his pillow to her.

He felt her arms still around him. It was as if no time had passed and they had just met. His body ached for her. His heart craved her approval. And he knew he would ride to the end of the earth, if necessary, to see her smile again. He left her there and wasted no time, taking the back stairs to the servants' quarters at a trot. Once there, he walked down the hall, rapping on doors as he went. As a line of heads poked into the hall, he issued terse instructions to Aston and the footmen for a systematic search of the house. Then he lit a lantern and proceeded out through the kitchen doors, towards the stables.

He doubted that the boy could have got far. But he could cover the ground faster on horseback. God forbid, if he should have to return with an injured child, speed might be of the essence.

Or perhaps he would not have to look far at all. As he approached his stallion's stall, Gerry could hear Satan raging over something. The sharp cries of an angry horse tore the stillness of the night, punctuated by iron-shod hooves slamming at the back wall of a stall, as though the occupant meant to kick it down.

He quickened his pace, yanking the door wide open and holding his light high so that he might see. There, at the back of the dimly lit enclosure, was Stewart, huddled in the corner, arms over his face waiting for the inevitable.

Gerry hung the lantern on a nail in the wall and stepped forward, grabbing a bridle in one hand and swinging the crook of his other arm over the rising and falling neck. He pushed with his full weight into the shoulder, sending a steady string of curses into the pointed black ear. In response the animal backed away from the boy and ceased his plunging. When Gerry felt he was calm enough, he fastened the harness and looped the reins over a ring in the wall.

Then he turned his attention to the boy, grabbing him by the collar of his coat and lifting him bodily from the stall. 'What the devil was the meaning of that?' he shouted into the small white face before him.

He had used a tone that had terrified more

than a few grown men. But the child dangling in front of him glared back and said, in a cold, clear voice, 'You cannot talk to me in that way. You are not my father.'

Gerry set him on his feet with a thump and reached for the lantern, holding it up to get a better look at the boy. He was dirty and trembling, but uninjured. But the look in his eyes was more than fear. Gerry had seen that mix of anger, betrayal and despair in the face of his enemies, just before the end. He had not let it stay his hand then and he showed no sympathy now. 'I will talk to you any way I choose, especially when you do something so foolish as to frighten your mother by running off in the middle of the night. Now what in blazes makes you think I am not your father?'

'Uncle Ronald told me, before he left. He said my father was a drunkard and a wastrel. He was a bad man and I would be a bad man, too.' The boy gave a sniff and his shoulders shuddered. But he did not cry. He was staring up at Gerry, as if waiting to be corrected. 'Uncle Ronald said Mama was ashamed to have me and that was why she lied. And that is why you hate me and want to send me away.'

It was not all true. But it was true enough that he could not just deny it. Even if he did, the child would never be free of the doubt. 'Why did you come here, instead of to me or your mother?'

'If Mama lied to me before,' he said, 'she would lie to me again. And you do not want me.'

'But why here?' Gerry repeated, more gently.

The boy's voice dropped to a whisper.

'Uncle Ronald said that no son of yours could be afraid of horses. And I am. So that would mean...' There was a long, dangerous pause. 'But maybe, if I could learn not to be afraid...'

'So you decided to lose your fear in the middle of the night, with a horse that has killed almost as many men as I have?' He shook his head in disbelief. 'Do you know what might have happened if I had not come along when I did?'

'He... He would have killed me.' The boy was whispering again. 'Because he knows I don't belong here.'

'He would have killed you because he has been trained to kick and bite at anything in front of him,' Gerry corrected. 'Satan is no ordinary horse. A dragoon's mount must be as ferocious as he is. Fearless of the carnage around him, the smell of blood and the beasts like himself dying on every side. He is ready to kick, bite and trample the enemy, if called to do so. He would have made short work of you, had I not come along.'

And thank God he had. If he had decided to search on foot, he'd have never found the boy. The next morning, the stable boys would have discovered the broken, bloody body at the feet of the stallion. That thought had him more frightened than he'd been since Waterloo.

'If he is just a mean horse, then it is not me.'

'It is not you,' Gerry agreed. 'And a love of horses is not something that appears magically in the blood. I did not always like them. When I was your age, I preferred to hide in the conservatory and pretend I was hunting tigers.' He thought for a moment. 'Of course, I do not like hunting either.' But he'd thought, perhaps if he tried hard enough, he could change.

'You hid in the conservatory? That is what I do. Does that mean I am yours after all?' Stewart was staring at him with such desperate hope that the lie was almost out of Gerry's mouth before he could stop it. Was this how it had been for poor Lily? When faced with an innocent child who had no share of blame in all that had happened, where was the virtue in honesty?

At last, he shook his head. 'Your father was a bad man. But so is your Uncle Ronald for telling you something your mother did not wish you to know.'

The first tears were streaking through the muck on the boy's cheeks. 'Who was he? And why didn't she tell me? How can I be someone else's, if she is married to you?'

What was he to say to this? The more questions he answered, the more there would be. He thought for a moment. 'It was something that happens sometimes, when a man is very bad and a woman is very beautiful. It happened because I was not here to stop it. It hurt your mother and frightened her badly. I suspect she didn't tell anyone, not even you, because she was still frightened, even after all this time.'

'She needn't be,' Stewart said, a little of his spirit returning. 'I was here to protect her.'

'You did a good job,' Gerry agreed. 'But now that will be my job.'

'And that's why you will send me to school,' Stewart finished for him. 'Because Mama does not need me, now that you are here.'

'Your mother still needs you,' he admitted. 'She told me so. But I think she might need me as well. Perhaps it would be better if we remain together, so that your mother can be safe and happy.' When one considered it, it was the only logical answer.

For the first time that evening, Stewart smiled. And then, the smile faded. 'But I am not your son.'

'Not by blood, perhaps.' The truth was forming in his head, even as he spoke. 'On the day we met, you told me that you like mathematics.'

The boy nodded, confused.

'You have not learned about them yet. But in mathematics, there is a thing called a proof. You can use a series of facts to prove another.'

The boy nodded again, trying to understand.

'If you are your mother's son, and I am your mother's husband, then I am your father. *Quod erat demonstrandum.*' His professors at Cambridge would have been appalled at the faulty logic. But the boy seemed satisfied with it. And much to his surprise, Gerry felt better than he had in days.

He stared down at the child again. 'Now that we have settled that, I trust that there will be no more trips to the stables to prove your worth under the hooves of my horse.'

The boy shook his head.

'And I suppose you are still afraid.' He didn't wait for an answer. The boy's fear was still obvious.

'To come here was not very sensible.' Then he grinned. 'But your mother will tell you that it was not very sensible for me to join the army. She thought I was going to die.'

'But you were a hero,' Stewart said, his eyes round.

'I was lucky. Just as you were tonight.'

'Wiscombes are lucky,' Stewart said.

'That they are,' Gerry agreed. 'Now stand out of the way.' He gestured the boy out into the aisle and led the horse out of the stall. Then he mounted the bare back.

When he looked down, the boy had plastered himself to the wall. He leaned over and held out an arm. 'Come here.'

Hesitantly, Stewart stepped forward into his reach and Gerry pulled him up to sit in front of him on the horse. 'You are perfectly safe, as long as I am here. Now let us go back to the house and set your mother's mind at rest.'

Chapter Twenty-Four

Lily stood alone in the hall, her face pressed against the window glass. Gerald was naïve if he thought that she would wait in the comfort of his bed while her son was God knew where. The house was awake. Every candle had been lit. And the servants had found nothing, just as she'd known they would.

Stewart was out there, somewhere. It was dark. So very dark. How could he see to avoid the hazards? Boars. Bears. Packs of wild dogs. All the creatures that roamed the forest at night could see better in the dark than a boy, even if he had taken a lantern. They could run faster as well.

But there were other things just as bad. If he was not found, someone would have to check the cistern. And the well. 'God,' she murmured aloud. 'Do not let it be that.'

Then she saw a distant light approaching the house. It was swinging with a strange gait and seemed too high to be held by a walking man.

It was a man on a horse. She tugged the door open and shouted into the night, 'Gerry! Did you find him?'

The horse galloped the last few yards to stop easily in front of her. Gerry smiled down at her. 'I told you not to worry.' Then he opened his coat to reveal her darling boy, astride a horse and nestled close to her husband.

She held out her arms and Gerry lowered him to the ground. And for a moment she was too relieved to speak. She could do nothing but hug him tight to her, until he squirmed in embarrassment. Then she let him go long enough to scold. 'Do not ever do that to me again, running away in the middle of the night, frightening the life out of the whole household.'

'I won't, Mama. I promise. And Papa says that tomorrow he will buy me a pony.'

'You are right you won't, young man. You will not be able to...' Then, her mind began to decipher what he was saying. His papa? A pony? He had arrived home in Gerry's arms and on a horse. But that had to be from necessity.

She looked to her husband for the answer and he gave her one of his infuriatingly charming, lopsided grins, paired with half a shrug. And under it all ran a childish descant about how ponies were small and safe and gentle and no different from big dogs. And who was silly enough to be afraid of a big dog?

The spots began to appear before her eyes again. And as the world swayed, she heard the command to 'Breathe, Lillian.' As she obeyed, his hands caught her under the arms and lifted her to her feet.

'Miss…'

'Fisher, Captain.' Aston supplied the name, *sotto voce*.

'Miss Fisher. Wash this boy. He has been playing in the stables and smells like a pony himself. I do not mind. But others might.'

'Yes, Captain.'

'And I am sorry for the inconvenience to you all, as is young Stewart. He will tell you so in the morning. Perhaps a glass of warm milk will help him back to sleep.'

'Of course, Captain.' Mrs Fitz was there and ready.

'And the rest of you? Back to sleep. Breakfast will be late tomorrow, since we will all be celebrating the quiet of an empty house.'

The staff gave a murmur of approval and one of the maids yawned and then giggled.

'Night, Mama.'

Lily felt a tug on her skirt and a kiss on her hand, but by the time she turned to look Stewart was inside the house and halfway up the stairs. The servants were dispersing as well. By the time she'd caught her breath and regained her wits, she was alone on the steps with her husband, who was still grinning.

'What happened?'

His smile faded. 'He knows. Ronald told him before he left.'

She had thought that the night could not be worse. Her breath was gone again as she imagined her son's shock and his anger at her betrayal.

'Breathe.' This time, it was not a command.

Just a gentle whisper against her temple. He was not simply holding her up. He was cradling her against him, swaying slightly as if they were dancing. 'I explained things to him as best I could. There will be more questions, of course.'

'I must go to him.' She started to pull away.

He pulled her back. 'Not tonight. He is settled now. Halfway back to bed, I should think. I thought diversionary tactics would serve better than a full account of how he came to be.'

'A diversion?' She smiled. 'The pony.'

'Exactly. There will be time enough tomorrow to talk about the past. I will help, if I can.'

'Tomorrow?' She had thought they would be packed and gone by evening.

He leaned away so she could see his smile, which was gentle. 'He and I discussed matters between us. We decided it might be best for you if we all lived together. Then we might both love and care for you without the inconvenience of distance.'

'But… Love… Are you sure?' Perhaps he cared for her. But much as she wanted it, the three of them living together sounded like an uneasy truce, at best.

'You said before that I hated Stewart. He said the same.' He was still smiling, but now his grey eyes looked sad. 'It is foolish to hate a small child who has done nothing more to me than exist.' He thought for a moment. 'I hate his father, of course. Both for who he was and for what he did to you. But the boy has done nothing in his life to deserve such a parent.'

'All I wanted was for him to have a father he could admire,' she admitted. 'That was why I lied.'

'Not all of us can have a hero.' Gerry said. 'My father was a harsh man. I cannot say I liked him, or agreed with his hobbies. But neither would I say that I was better off without him. I am not as perfect as the man you were hoping for. But your son needs a father. I can be that for him.'

'I never doubted it,' she replied. But these sounded like rationalisations of a difficult situation. 'But some day, you will want children of your own.'

'Many,' he agreed. 'And soon.'

'If you acknowledge Stewart, he will stand in their way to inheritance.'

'What I want does not really matter. There is

no way of knowing how many children we might have,' he reminded her. 'For all we know, there might be none. But there is no entail on the property. All could share equally.'

It was the sort of solution she'd longed for since the moment Stewart had been born. But now that it was here, it was all too sudden. If it was but a ploy to keep her, it would not be enough to secure Stewart's future. 'I would like nothing better than that we could all be together as a family,' she said, touching his cheek. 'But why now? What has changed that you would allow it?'

'Just now, I pulled your son from Satan's stall. He risked death from a beast that terrified him, trying to prove his worth to himself and to me.' And now, the brave Captain Wiscombe had to stop to swallow his emotion. 'I will not let that happen again. The boy was born here, and he stays here.' He hugged her roughly to him, as if the contact would give him the strength to master himself.

She hugged him back, for it was clear that he had finally seen Stewart for who he was and not just a horrible mistake. 'You will not regret this. Once you have got to know him, you will find he is so very much like you that he could be your own.'

'Like me?' He laughed.

'He is like you on the day you proposed. Sweet and earnest. Ready to conquer the world, with no thought to what might go wrong. You were a hero in the making, Captain Wiscombe. It just took time for your true character to be revealed.' She smiled and kissed him on the cheek to show him how dear he was to her.

'As I remember it, you were convinced that I was a fool and marching to my death,' he said, nuzzling her hair.

'You proved me wrong,' she reminded him.

'As you did me, about young Stewart. And for your information, the boy is more like you. Smart. Stubborn. Fearless.'

'And utterly devoted to you,' she added.

'Most important, he is a part of you. Since I love you to the last fibre of your being, I will love and honour your child, and make him my own.' The kiss that followed was long and slow, and soothed the last of her worries about the future.

'And I love you, Gerry Wiscombe,' she said with a sigh. 'More each day since the moment I met you.'

He was smiling again. 'I've dreamed of you saying those words almost as long.'

'My father and brother said you married me because you were smitten with me. I did not believe them. You had other plans for your future, even from the first.'

'You will have to take my word for it. I was smitten. I still am.' He grinned. 'And I had other plans. I still do.'

'What are they?' she asked.

'To teach our son that horses are not to be feared. To live out the rest of my life quietly at Wiscombe Chase, surrounded by my loving family.' Then he looked down at her, mischief in his eyes. 'But first, I mean to bed my wife.'

Before she could answer, he had scooped her up, tossed her over his shoulder and was carrying her up the stairs to their room.

* * * * *

MILLS & BOON®

Why shop at millsandboon.co.uk?

Each year, thousands of romance readers find their perfect read at millsandboon.co.uk. That's because we're passionate about bringing you the very best romantic fiction. Here are some of the advantages of shopping at www.millsandboon.co.uk:

* **Get new books first**—you'll be able to buy your favourite books one month before they hit the shops

* **Get exclusive discounts**—you'll also be able to buy our specially created monthly collections, with up to 50% off the RRP

* **Find your favourite authors**—latest news, interviews and new releases for all your favourite authors and series on our website, plus ideas for what to try next

* **Join in**—once you've bought your favourite books, don't forget to register with us to rate, review and join in the discussions

Visit **www.millsandboon.co.uk**
for all this and more today!